T0340501

mamele

Also by Gemma Reeves

Victoria Park

mamele

gemma reeves

THE BOROUGH PRESS

The Borough Press
An imprint of HarperCollins*Publishers* Ltd
1 London Bridge Street
London SE1 9GF

www.harpercollins.co.uk

HarperCollins*Publishers*
Macken House,
39/40 Mayor Street Upper,
Dublin 1
D01 C9W8
Ireland

First published by HarperCollins*Publishers* Ltd 2024
1

A catalogue record for this book is available from the British Library.

The quotation on page 167 is from a sermon by Rabbi Sheila Shulman, originally
published by Pronoun Press in *Watching for the Morning* (2007).

ISBN: 978-0-00-865818-2 (HB)
ISBN: 978-0-00-865819-9 (TPB)

Typeset in Adobe Garamond Pro
by Palimpsest Book Production Ltd, Falkirk, Stirlingshire

Printed and bound in the UK using 100% Renewable Electricity
by CPI Group (UK) Ltd

For my son

ONE

'Hi, Edie,' my sister says.

I twist the phone cord between my fingers. 'Hi, Sissy.'

She takes a breath. 'I just wanted to see if you changed your mind. There's plenty of space at ours. It's not too late.'

'I know,' I say. 'And no. I haven't changed my mind.'

Every Sunday, Simone calls at 11 a.m. This has been the routine for the last decade. There have been only two occasions when Simone has rung outside of our allotted hour. Once when our mother was diagnosed with breast cancer, the other when Simone's daughter was born. Today is Friday but I'm not alarmed: I know why my sister is calling. Tomorrow is our mother's eightieth birthday.

Simone sighs and the sigh turns into a hacking cough. My sister had flu last week and I've been worried about her, although I guess not worried enough to call and check.

'Still no better?' I ask.

'I'm fine,' she says, 'but Zelda's getting worse. This might be your last chance.'

'Last chance for what? At this rate she'll outlive us both.'

Simone laughs and then coughs again. 'God forbid.' She pauses to blow her nose. 'Are you sure?'

'She would hate for me to be there and you know it. Besides, it's Stella's birthday tonight. We're having a big dinner here. I can't get away. Call me Sunday.'

Despite my nonchalance on the phone, part of me can't believe my mother has made it to such a grand old age. The other part has been plagued by a terrible feeling something will go wrong on this milestone birthday. My mother likes to incite drama. Blow things up. It is her favourite pastime.

With my mother and me, it all comes down to this: I have not wanted to understand her and she has not wanted to understand me. Simone tells me about my mother's life when she calls each week. But the exchange of information is one way. I haven't seen my mother in thirty-seven years. I am dead to her.

Over time, thoughts of my mother have quietened, dampening away to the occasional twitch. But all week long, memories of my childhood have returned to me, as vivid and slippery as slices of canned peach. I am sick on that syrup. Daily, now, her voice pools in my ears. Fragments, sometimes just syllables, the cadence of the old language. I try and try but I cannot escape her shadow presence. I carry her on my back.

Some of these memories take shapes I do not always recognise. There are things I simply could not have known.

It's as if I've inherited my mother's memories and they are passing themselves off as my own.

How like Zelda if this is the case: my life the train that rumbles over her tracks.

The first time my mother left me alone to go and watch a film at the Kilburn Empire Theatre I was nine months old. She put me down in my high-sided cot; milk-happy, I closed my eyes obligingly. I dreamed I'd returned to my mother's body and watched the world through the drum of her stomach. I saw: the restless churning of the Black Sea; fish guts sliding between her finger and thumb; fragrant, creamy white blossoms tumbling from black locust trees. It was so windy in Odessa. It was nothing like Maida Vale.

Meanwhile, my mother gathered her things. Leather gloves, hat, handbag, keys. Yardley red lipstick and blotting papers. She hovered in the doorway, then kissed my sleeping cheek. 'Be a good girl, Edie,' she murmured, and left for a matinee showing of Leslie Arliss's *The Wicked Lady*. When I read her diary fifteen years later I saw she scored it seven out of ten. It was the most popular film of 1946.

Because I wasn't howling when my mother returned, just wide-eyed, blinking at the ceiling, she deemed her expedition a success and frequently left the flat without me.

She did not tell my father, who was busy working at the Spanish Embassy.

Sometimes I slept peacefully. Other times I tried to find my feet, snatching at the air around my toes. Occasionally I screamed and screamed, puffing out my cheeks in rage. My little body tensed, then gave up.

This continued until Mrs Damsky, our widowed neighbour, finally cottoned on and confronted my mother.

Zelda, are you crazy? What kind of woman leaves her baby? Where are you going? To another man?

'No, no!' my mother replied. 'I just want some time alone.'

Were the bonds between the women of our block strong enough to keep such a secret, or did Mrs Damsky rat on my mother and tell my father? Was it the first of many explosive rows to come? I never got to ask.

After this episode, my mother brought down the full force of her personality on our neighbour, who did not acknowledge me again until I was a toddler rolling marbles down our shared corridor, delighting in their undulant colours, the clunk as they ricocheted off the walls.

'Stop!' she yelled from her doorway. 'Just stop, you horrible child.'

It was here I had my first inkling that I was a bad seed which had bloomed, violently, from my mother's body – a feeling that intensified years later, the night my mother discovered I was in love with a girl. When she thrust a suitcase into my trembling hands and told me to leave, I had no idea it was the last time we'd ever set eyes on each other. I was sixteen years old.

When I was a child, my mother schooled me in the ways of keeping house. She taught me how to be a *baleboste*. *A good woman is a good housewife*, she would say, preparing me for the life I was expected to lead. A life like hers. Today Joanna has asked me to clean the house from top to bottom. Some things just stick, no matter where you go.

No one likes Stella but I've still got to clean the house for her. No, that's not fair. Joanna likes her eldest daughter. They are the spitting image of each other. When I say spitting image, I mean they share genetics and a plastic surgeon. Stella wears slinky dresses where you can see the half-moon scars at the curve of her breasts. Lift the hair that covers Joanna's ears and there are the incision marks. Two peas. In our own image. All that.

Joanna is out buying food and then she will spend an hour at the hairdresser. When Harry was alive, Joanna needed nothing from me but sex and a little light house-keeping. Harry had given her a home and two children and freedom to be herself, which is to say freedom to be beautiful, maintain that beauty, perform that beauty – both privately (to him) and publicly (to his friends and colleagues). Harry has been dead for years but she still keeps her end of the bargain. I am expected to keep mine.

Damson Manor was once very impressive. Its size still astounds me even after two decades living here. Six double bedrooms, three bathrooms and one downstairs toilet, reception hall, study, two living rooms, a brick wine vault, the conservatory where no one likes to sit, and my favourite room – the kitchen, with its floating island and a long velvet banquette. All décor decisions were made before my arrival and so nothing has been designed to my taste or convenience. It's the small things you notice, like how far the toaster is from the fridge when it should be closer to be near the butter.

Now there's only the two of us, Joanna and I ping-pong between rooms, filling the space with cigarette smoke. It's more than two people could ever hope to use. Only the dogs take full advantage of the house, bounding from room to room making beds of couches and lazing beneath the piano no one plays.

I snap on Marigolds, pull out the bucket of cleaning products from under the stairs. I sink my hands into every nook and cranny, running a sponge across each flaking windowsill; drag a cloth along the dark lines of the paint-work, watch dirt roll and gather into little pearls. I tackle the stains beneath the sticky washing-up bottles, the burnt crumbs beside and on top of the toaster, the claggy remnants baked into the rings of the hob. I even descale the kettle. Under Joanna's instruction, I try to remove every trace of our grubby existence. The days we do not dress, the days we smoke multiple packets of Marlboro, the days we spend drinking the good stuff still left in the cellar. It takes hours and my joints ache. Filth permeates this old house. It's written into every surface, the private morphology of our lives.

I address the dining room last. Mop the floors, soap the perennial paw prints on the flagstone tiles. Heave and strain against the furniture, seek out motes under the couch which have been pushed into neat rows by my repetitive vacuuming. Beneath an armchair: a stray Scrabble tile – the letter M. Two points. M for me. M for mine.

Yet nothing here is mine. Not a single piece of furniture. No paintings, none of the many ceramics. My clothes take up a quarter of the expansive wardrobes. There is just one suitcase on a high shelf in which my expired passport, my father's watch and a few photographs can be found. Joanna calls me her second husband. Perhaps she thinks it's endearing but it irks me since I'm wed to nothing. I've long made peace with what little belongs to me. I know what is not mine intimately. In this way things are lighter, freer. It has taught me to be patient about the contours of a life.

I give the mantlepiece a final once-over and break a vase in my haste. It was a memento of a trip Joanna and Harry went on in the winter of '89. I stayed at home, looked after the dogs. The girls were at boarding school. Mild concern about Joanna's reaction, but then mostly annoyance. Shards everywhere. *What a yutz*, I hear my mother say.

All this cleaning might seem like an erasure, but it's the opposite. I assert myself in the clean spaces I leave behind. Here is my reflection in the stovetop. Here I am peering into the glass coffee table. I even like my cleaning clothes: an old pair of Harry's denim overalls. But, despite all my efforts, nothing will ever make the paintwork look fresh again, banish the damp, close the gaps between the floorboards, conceal the cigarette burns in the carpet and on the couch.

I stop to eat a Brie baguette, devour it standing by the sink so that the crumbs drop straight into the plughole and I don't ruin my hard work. The doughy centre is so delicious I rush the meal and scratch the roof of my mouth. I stare out of the kitchen's round window and across the grounds, tennis courts to the left, empty swimming pool to the right. De-cushioned sun loungers, white skeletons exposed. The wind has knocked over the pampas grass in the garden. The stems bow in the breeze, bent into awkward yoga positions or maybe they are just crippled. Blackberry bushes curve along the fence and I feel unreasonable loss looking at the bare brambles, recalling their summer bounty. The net curtain shifts against the wall, the cold of the day coming in.

I haven't tackled the bedrooms, but fuck it, I call for the dogs anyway. They come bounding as fast as old beasts can go. Mitzi, Coco and Betsey: two Spanish greyhounds and our pampered Afghan hound. Far too many dogs for the old women Joanna and I are becoming.

The gravel crunches underfoot as I make my way down the wide driveway, the dogs skittering ahead. It used to be landscaped, all topiary and sculpted hedges; flowers arranged in their beds. But Joanna and I don't tend to the plants. There's no money left for a gardener; we've probably spent it on Beaujolais. The winter sun pierces through low clouds and the grass is striped with afternoon shadows, the leaves so golden they look wet – almost molten – in the light. It's beautiful, I suppose, but they are shrinking too, shrivelling and crisping, the last ones ready to fall from the branch.

The dogs halt at the Land Rover, turn impatiently to where I lag behind looking at the doors to the old coach house. In the sunlight, the scrubbed graffiti shines anew. *Pussy Puncher*, it says. Short and sweet, the words' bite depleted by how archaic the expression has become. Yet it still has power, still holds the echo of violence from local kids who heard rumours about what went on here at the weekends.

It's a ten-minute drive to Broadstairs beach where I take the dogs for their walk. They know the routine and jump into the back seats, which are covered with an expensive fleece caked in mud and sand from yesterday's walk, and the one before that. The act of washing it has become a joke: it's just another thing I can never get clean. Besides, I like the faint smell of the sea that clings to it.

There are a few other blank-eyed houses set back from the road, grand and falling apart like ours. Portico entrances, stone-pillared verandas, dry wisteria vines. All surrounded by their own versions of high clipped hedges, juniper bushes, maple trees. Everything has been planted and then groomed to keep prying eyes at bay. But I don't know whose eyes – the road is so quiet, and it's been a long time since the sound of visitors arriving from London has disturbed anyone. A long time since the police have been called.

The engine gives its guttural humph, the dogs' tails thump against the seat, and Schopenhauer blares out from the stereo. I shuffle through the disc-changer until Dusty announces herself. I serenade the dogs, slip on purple-tinted aviators, wind down the window and let the wind blast my curls. I pass the petrol station, the post office. Nothing else to see, no other cars. I slow as I round the bends, leaning into them like I'm on the back of a motor-cycle, like I'm not a middle-aged woman driving a dead man's car through the English countryside.

Broadstairs is surrounded by seven bays with white chalk cliffs. They protrude from the landscape like baby teeth breaking out of raw pink gums. I park, pay, and then clip leads to the dogs' collars. We walk along the clifftop to Botany Bay, the dogs straining and panting, desperate to run. Everything below us is beige and wet. The ocean crashes, white foam layering on white foam. I let the dogs off the leash early and they skitter down the stone stairs and spring onto the sand.

Only the dog walkers and the diehard locals brave the beach in winter. A couple of young mothers push prams along the promenade, trying to lull their screaming wards to sleep. I keep rubber balls in the deep pockets of my windbreaker and throw them in a manic one-person three-beast relay. One ricochets off a beach bin, hits the centre of the Broadstairs coat of arms with its Latin motto *Stella Maris*, Star of the Sea, a derivative of which all local pubs use for their names.

The wind is brutal, roaring with urgency, pummelling my skin with salt. The water makes a ferocious noise, white foam multiplying by the minute. I linger by the ocean edge and let the wind whip at me, strip out the layers of grime and dirt that still cling to my skin, wait for it to sweep away my mood and my memories. But there is a crack in me somewhere and through it enters the voice of my mother.

When my mother washed my hair she crooned, *mamele*, *mamele*, into my ear. Little mother, meaning little daughter, meaning you're a good girl, Edie. She worked shampoo through my curls, fingers firm and insistent. My mother's body was thick but her hands were slender and she turned her palms to protect my eyes as she rinsed the suds with a bucket of water. I let my eyes flutter open anyway, watched the droplets fall from the tangled tips of my hair.

'All done,' she said, standing me up and towelling down my body, rubbing dry each patch of skin as if making sure it was still there. '*Abi gezunt*,' she said. *As long as you're healthy, you can be happy.* She told me it didn't matter I looked just like my father. I would grow into my face. Maybe my skin would lighten to her shade – such changes were not unheard of.

I squinted at my mother's features. Dark eyes set deep in the folds of her face, thick eyebrows, a large but elegant nose, a full mouth always painted red. The palest skin. It was a great misfortune to have a mother who looked so different from me, who wished I looked less like myself.

17

While I bathed, my mother liked to tell me stories about my life. Mostly they were stories I didn't know first-hand, from times I was too young to remember. How I'd behaved when my first tooth arrived (badly), or how she'd felt while watching my first crawl (so proud!). She especially liked the one where she noticed the birthmark on my *tuchus* had disappeared (the saddest day). But my mother's favourite story took place before I was even born, in a space of exquisite longing. This one, she told over and over again.

'We tried for an age before you came along,' she said, drying between each of my toes with a maroon towel. 'I thought there was something wrong with me. Why couldn't I conceive? Of course, my first worry was that I had slighted God by marrying your *goyam* father and this was my punishment – no matter his conversion. I thought I was going the way of Sarah or Rachel or Rebecca. So, I prayed for my own blessing. I tried all the old remedies, ate as much fish and garlic as I could lay my hands on. Oh, how I went out of my mind. Out of my mind! How hollow I was.'

She slipped a cotton nightgown over my head and sat me on the edge of the tub to comb through my curls. 'When you finally arrived, what *mitzvah*! And then, the shock! What was this alien thing, squirming, all needing, all helpless? But your father and I, we covered your round belly with kisses. We whispered promises to the soles of your wriggling feet, your *tuchus*, your upturned nose. We asked God to keep you safe.'

I listened, warm and drowsy from my bath, soothed by the repetition of these promises, as if each time she spoke the words they stretched out their roots in newly fertile soil.

Now I wonder which God, my mother's or my father's, witnessed those vows? I'd like to know who covered their ears.

The light is already fading, the sky sagging over the horizon. Joanna's car isn't in the driveway.

I drop my keys into the dish on the sideboard and rush to the downstairs bathroom. If only I could be like the dogs, urinating freely along the pavement. My stream hits the porcelain with a vengeance – the only sound until the scuttle of paws on wood as the dogs clamber upstairs to sleep off the afternoon's excitement. Relief settles in my belly and when I lean back, I notice my psoriasis cream has moved from one end of the bathtub to the other which means Kiki, Joanna's youngest, is already here. When she visits, she smothers the soles of her feet in the stuff, slips on cotton socks and goes to bed that way. She says it soothes the dead skin, heals the cracks, and when she wakes her feet are newborn soft. Never mind my own skin, tight, red-raw and flaking. I pop the lid and examine the pot. Her fingertips have left rivulets in the emollient like ski trails.

There are a lot of good things about Kiki – how she's nothing like her sister Stella, for starters – but I've never felt remotely like her stepmother. I'm not convinced Joanna feels like her mother, either. As far as I can tell, Joanna regarded child-rearing as destiny, not desire. She shipped both girls off to boarding school as soon as she could. So long, be good, grow up well.

I find Kiki upstairs, lying face down on the floor of her old bedroom. She is completely still save for her chest rising and falling. The Velvet Underground is on the turntable, turned down low. Doug Yule sings 'Candy Says' and immediately I'm back in a Soho bar flirting with a stranger so they'd buy me a whiskey sour and offer me a Pall Mall in the years before I met Joanna. Kiki's beaded orange kaftan adds to the impression of time collapsed. I ask what she's doing. The response is muffled; I try again. Kiki raises her head. Her hair is naturally blonde but she bleaches it anyway until the ends become hay. A barber turned it into a ragged crop recently and now it's licked back with gel.

Finally she says, 'Smelling the pine of the floorboards.'

The corner of her lip is still touching the wood. Kiki is only twenty-three but that's still too old for this shit. I check my watch. 4.50 p.m. 'Little early to be high, isn't it?'

'Hah,' she says, like air bleeding from a radiator.

Warm light diffuses through a square of muslin covering a lampshade. In the fireplace, milky white church candles melt into one another. Their bodies fuse as separate wicks flicker. I join Kiki on the floor and stare up at the ceiling. A patch of mould blooms in the right-hand corner. I study it until it begins to pulsate. I snap my eyes shut, turn my face to the wood. The pine does smell good. 'The mould is pulsating,' I say.

Kiki rolls onto her side, giggles, and then stretches a long arm towards my hair. 'Are you baked, too?'

I laugh. 'Your eyes.'

She gives me that melty smile of hers. One front tooth reaches across to kiss the other. I love that she's never fixed it. 'Your everything,' she says, and then I feel each crease on my face as if it's been sliced with a fine blade. She plays with my curls, pulling at each one before letting it spring back. 'I'm so glad you grew out the mullet,' she murmurs. 'How is your hair still so black?'

'My father's genes.' This slips out of my mouth easily, as if I knew how he looked in later life. 'He was very handsome.'

When I was a child, my father's appearance was a relief to me. I could see myself in his features in a way I couldn't with my mother. There was a particular photograph of him I loved above the fireplace in Carlton Mansions. In it, he wore a linen capri suit and a white shirt with the top button undone. The fabric was slightly crumpled, with a faint front crease down the middle of his trousers. The jacket sat on his shoulders, arms free, as if it had been dropped on him from above. I've taken a lot of inspiration from my father's fashion over the years, especially those outfits from the 30s and 40s. In the photo he was holding some object I could never make out – a thin pen or pencil, perhaps. Although his gaze was beyond the camera, there was something certain, not wistful, about his look.

Something grounded. My mother said the photo was taken in his birthplace, Astoria – you can just make out the mountains on the horizon – a month before he moved to London and met my mother. Now when I think of that image I know he was envisaging a future that did not include me.

Shadows move across the ceiling and all of a sudden: full dark outside. The record ends. Static fuzz floats over the speaker. Kiki rolls onto her stomach and pushes herself onto her hands and knees. She inhales and rounds her spine, exhales and lets her spine dip. She stands and opens the door.

'Mummy's back from the fishmonger,' she says, yawning. She closes the door again and walks to the sideboard. 'Lobsters terrify me. Do you know they taste with their legs? And they have a tiny set of teeth in their stomachs to chew food.'

Lobster thermidor is one of Joanna's signature dishes, a treat she used to make for parties back when expense wasn't an issue. I used to enjoy eating shellfish because it was forbidden to me as a child. But in truth, bottom feeders give me the creeps. All that scuttling. Hard shells rubbing along ocean crust in the dark. Perhaps I've never been able to forget my mother's warning: *Keep Kashrut, Edie. The Old Testament says eat only fish with fins and scales. Do you want to burn in hell?* It's always her mixed messages I recall most often, the way she liked to borrow fear and guilt from my father's renounced Catholicism to bolster the identity she built around her own religion.

There's the fizz of a lighter sparking and then the musk of pot. Kiki inhales – one second, two seconds, three seconds – then exhales. 'I can't face Stella without . . . something,' she says.

'Mmm,' I agree. 'I could have used something earlier to talk to Simone.'

'How is your sister?'

I explain she had the flu last week but she's on the mend and then I go quiet, touched by the question. Although we talk on the phone weekly, I haven't actually seen my sister in twenty years, not since the one time she visited Damson Manor and it ended in disaster. Simone leads a very normal life in north London with her husband and daughter, Anais. Normal, save for our mother, whom she collects from Maida Vale each Saturday lunchtime and brings back to her flat. They eat, watch TV, and our mother tells Simone how she's tired of living. That she cannot walk. That she doesn't expect to live more than a month. She is going blind. Her heart is fluttering like a little bird and will cease to beat at any moment. In response, Simone reminds our mother that she is in perfect health. That she is almost eighty and takes no medication. That she is doing unreasonably well. In the early evening, Simone drives her home, where our mother manages to walk the two flights of stairs to her flat, unaided, with the light steps of a teenage girl in love.

I like Simone – I might even love her like a sister should. She does not deserve to deal with our mother alone, but that wasn't my choice.

Kiki squats low and the folds of her kaftan puddle over her feet. She offers the joint and I accept even though it will piss off Joanna. I take a long drag and feel so good so quickly that I laugh.

'Purple Haze,' Kiki says. 'Ryan's new strain from his greenhouse.'

'He's talented.'

She plays with a loose bead on her dress, rolling it between thumb and middle finger, teasing it from its thread. Gold bracelets wind up her wrist in snakish formation. The bead finally yields, and she flicks it away. She lays down again and drops an arm around my shoulder. I take another toke and pass it back, hold the smoke in my lungs and then send perfect smoke rings into the air. The second ring dissolves before the first.

Something sooty drops down the chimney into the fireplace, snuffing out a church candle. 'Shit,' Kiki says, her voice gentle, unbothered.

I ask if Ryan is joining us tonight. He works at an abattoir in Norfolk and visits Kiki in London on the weekends she isn't seeing her girlfriend. She blinks twice. I think it means yes.

'And Chloe?'

'Rome,' she says, eventually. 'Some pottery course.' She stares at the burning tip of the joint.

I press my palms face down on the floorboards and imagine I can feel the weight of every person who has stepped on this floor before me. Solid bodies and then a thousand ghostly feet. I think about Harry, who I almost never think about anymore. His heavy tread, his booming voice, his later odd behaviour which seemed kind of exciting at the time until we realised it was the cancer. His wet sticky breath at the end.

'I miss this house,' Kiki says.

I turn to face her, surprised. 'You hated it as a kid.'

'I was hardly here as a kid. When I was, I couldn't sleep.'

At that I feel bad. The house could have been the perfect place to raise children. When the girls were young there was an aviary, a stable with two horses and an orchard. The garden was magnificent. I remember the first time Joanna and Harry brought me here. It was summer. Fruits bobbled on the edge of branches. Music blared. There were people everywhere, so much laughter. Also: bowls of cocaine, sex sounds leaking through closed doors.

The room is suddenly too large and just as quickly – too small. I sit up to steady the feeling and train my attention on the wallpaper. It is cream with embossed fleur-de-lis – pretty once, now marred by stale smoke, curling corners and that passing of time that makes everything look outdated until it rolls back into fashion again. A damask throw covers the bed. I have no idea why there are so many plump pillows.

'I like to read in bed,' Kiki says, and I realise I've asked the question out loud.

I press my palm to my chest. 'Is your heart beating faster?'

'I think . . . maybe . . . slower. You know, at the abattoir they have an entire fridge just for hearts.'

'A fridge for hearts,' I say.

'You okay?' Kiki asks, pinging another curl away from my forehead.

'Just a headrush,' I say, scratching through my chinos to get at a psoriasis patch on my calf.

When I stand, each step disorients me. The room is so long it's like I'll never get to the end of it. If Kiki is too old for this shit what does that make me?

I scratch at my skin again. My body, as old as papyrus, creasing where once it moved with ease. How familiar physical discomfort has become.

'What's the deal with you and Ryan anyway?' I ask.

Kiki looks at me, her face suddenly serious. 'Total freedom,' she says.

My mother took me to synagogue with her as soon as I was deemed old enough to behave properly on the number six bus. We were members of the West London Synagogue on Upper Berkeley Street. Shabbat, evening service, was her preferred time of worship because it was the busiest. Work on our appearance began an hour before leaving. My mother gathered my hair into two French braids, murmuring *feh* and *fercockt* as the curls disobeyed her vision. She stuffed my body into a terrible tea dress with a Peter Pan collar. Scratchy skin, socks slipping, back dripping with sweat. No matter – we were there to be seen.

Worship seemed to have very little to do with God. My mother went to pass judgement on what the other women were wearing. This was easy to comment on because they were always out of earshot, avoiding her. She had Married Out. To the devout women my mother had betrayed the faith in the worst way. I knew this because she told me. 'In their eyes,' she said, 'you're but one step from a bastard.' I thought being a bastard sounded interesting.

The only women who were nice to my mother were those who lived in our building. There was Vera, Margery, Rivka and Dora. Like my mother, they'd all migrated during or after the war and ended up in Carlton Mansions in varying degrees of happy matrimony.

I didn't care for synagogue but I was seduced by the singing. The harmonising Hebrew moved me in a way English songs did not. What's more, I was actually good at it. My voice, which came from deep inside my chest and pushed out through my throat by way of some primordial realm or skein of velvet had a low burnished quality that only deepened with time. It was, to my mother's delight, exactly like the commanding voice of a rabbi who'd been born reciting the Talmud, the only occasion when being delicate slipped from its pedestal. When I sang, the melody lifted me up and out of my seat, out of my mother's grasp, and floated me high in the alcoves where I let the stained-glass windows blast coloured light through my constricted body. As a child, it was as close to freedom as I ever got.

In the gaps between singing, the services were long and I spent them trying to imagine my mother as a young child, dragged along to a synagogue in Odessa. All I knew about my mother's life before London was that she had come from a place with a black sea, and in my mind its inky water coloured everything with darkness. What else could explain my mother's moods? When she mentioned her homeland, it was with sighs and *kvetching*, flashing eyes and murmurs of horror. She had a story inside of her, churning around, blackening her lungs with that black water. I had never even seen the sea.

I tried to scrabble out of my tea dress the minute we were home. But there were so many buttons from the nape of my neck to the crack of my bottom, I couldn't get undressed without help.

I couldn't get out of those dresses and I couldn't get out of my childhood.

The house smells of melting cheese and butter. Joanna has the radio on: Handel at his most festive, hyperbolic. I watch in the kitchen doorway as she stirs the white sauce, a Marlboro Red smouldering in the crystal ashtray next to the pan.

Joanna turns. 'Darling,' she says, 'there you are.' She picks up her cigarette and ash falls to the floor. Joanna has been for a blow-dry and her platinum waves are brushed away from her face and set into an unmoving bob which teases her padded shoulders. I can smell the lacquer, its acrid floral residue. It's a variation of the same style she wore when we met and the creamy champagne is the most perfect shade of blonde I've ever encountered. She's wearing the Chanel bouclé skirt suit we bought in Harrods – a ridiculous outfit to be cooking in but then she has so many she isn't afraid of getting one dirty.

'We've got Ryan tonight, not the other one,' she says.

'Kiki told me. She's upstairs.'

Joanna frowns but where her forehead should crease into lines like mine, the skin merely puckers for a moment and then tightens again.

'Taste this.' She offers me her wooden spoon, the tip glossy with cheese sauce. It's rich and buttery with fresh tarragon and chives. Delicious. But I find eating at these dinners difficult. The girls do not see me as family. They call me *a friend of the family*. Sometimes if I open my mouth too wide to bite down on a chunk of food then the desire to say something inappropriate will rise up. I have to be careful. The back of my throat houses a lot of ill will.

Out of nowhere, rain pummels the windows. I turn the dials on the radio until a Prince song drowns it out. Joanna puts her wooden spoon face down on the countertop, tuts loudly, and switches it back to Classic FM. The radio DJ talks in the transition between songs. Inane chatter about the new millennium. The Y2K bug, the Dome, DVD replacing VHS. It's just another century. They roll around.

Joanna takes a chef's knife from a drawer and places it into my hand. The blade is long and sharp. She points at the six orange bodies on the kitchen island, still as marble, and then announces she's going to the wine cellar. I resign myself to dismantling the lobsters, first snapping away the claws, then cutting each body in half. I wash the head cavities under cold water, then dry them gently with kitchen roll. I'm still buzzing from Kiki's smoke and my hands are pleasantly detached, limbs moving through the familiar motions without my brain having to fire up. I lay the lobsters cut side up on a baking tray. I think I can smell the sea even though it's been boiled away. I get to work, cracking the claws and picking out the meat.

The first time I tried shellfish was with Joanna and

Harry. They took me to a Broadstairs restaurant, sat me between them, and ordered a *fruits de mer* and a bottle of Veuve Clicquot to toast our new union. The shellfish arrived on a silver platter, glinting, still slick with sea. Mussels and clams steamed open and exposed, dramatic crab claws, lengths of lobster, little knots of whelks and winkles; a langoustine belly up, beady eyes watching the ceiling. I took an oyster first, touched my tongue to the cold raw flesh. It was like licking another tongue. Harry laughed so I knocked it back, swallowing in one gulp as they'd instructed. I felt the thing slide down my throat, salty and curiously slimy. They each kissed one of my cheeks and poured more champagne.

I divide the lobster meat and pack the head cavities with the flesh, taking from one part of the crustacean and putting it back in another, until they're stuffed full.

'Bravo,' Joanna says, eyeing up my handiwork. I wash the muck from my hands. The water from the tap is always slightly yellow from the old lead pipes.

When the doorbell rings, the dogs go berserk.

Ryan greets me, slipping off his hood and stamping his feet on the welcome mat. Fat droplets of water run down his jacket. He bends and greets each of the dogs by name, letting them lick his wet hands. I stick my head out the door, pull it back in. The rain is so heavy the trees' branches sag. Ryan offers me a bleeding package of greaseproof paper. 'Couple of venison steaks and some extra treats,' he says.

Kiki clatters down the stairs in clogs, one hand gliding confidently over the loose bannisters which veer away from her grip. She must have splashed cold water over her face. Her skin sparkles. I am still so stoned.

She kisses Ryan on the mouth and then Joanna emerges from the kitchen. I leave them talking in the hallway to deposit the gifts and fetch Ryan a beer and Kiki a white wine spritzer.

The doorbell buzzes again. 'Happy birthday, my angel!' Joanna says. 'You look stunning.' The others murmur agreement, and then Stella's gravelly voice says, 'He flew to Qatar. Business.'

I join everyone in the dining room with the drinks and there is Stella, waist-length glossy blonde hair swinging, a cream silk shirt of such quality she may as well be wearing the price tag. She flashes me a perfunctory smile and then points at her overnight bag. 'Could you put this somewhere safe?'

I pick up the bag. It's heavy. And then I cannot help myself. 'No Kamil?'

She shakes her head and asks if we have any vodka. She knows there is always vodka.

'Right, I'm going to warm up the blinis,' Joanna says, and I realise she's bought caviar. I have no idea which credit card she could have used.

I leave the bag in the cupboard under the stairs where nobody will think to look for it, and then return to the kitchen. Joanna is heaping caviar with a mother of pearl spoon onto sour cream blinis until they carry a cluster of dilated pupils. She places the tray in my hands.

The table has been laid with the family Wedgewood,

each porcelain plate decorated with a blue and pink flower motif, Joanna's prized crystal wine glasses to their right. The room is glowing with light from the chandelier. You could almost miss the huge stain on the ceiling where Kiki flooded the bath years ago. I sail through the starters still swimmy with smoke and when that buzz runs out, I turn to the Chablis. We drain the first bottle, then the second by the time the lobsters are ready.

Joanna is in her element with her beautiful girls in the room. Stella modelled until she married Kamil – a significantly older oil tycoon. Kiki has never worked, but instead turns hobbies into consuming obsessions: first horses, then the cello, then an array of other artistic enterprises until she settled on painting and charmed her way into the Royal College of Art. In this room of prickly women, gentle Ryan holds his own, asking the right questions at the right moments, staying silent when necessary. All that work with death makes him very tactful with the living.

When I tune back in, Stella is asking her sister about art school.

'I had this experience the other day, with my professor,' Kiki says, 'kind of an epiphany. We were having a tutorial about my life drawing and he didn't like how I represented the female body. He said my strokes were too hard, too firm, like I was trying to impose a shape that wasn't there. And we talked about you, Mummy, about how I didn't see you very much as a child.' She stops to help herself to another serving of minted new potatoes. The butter drips down the spoon. 'And he thinks that's why I can't see the model as she is. Instead I see her as I want her to be, as like this figure of motherhood, all wide hips and round stomach. Large sagging breasts. Although obviously *your* breasts aren't like that, Mummy. Anyway, it's all wrong, you know. It's holding me back.'

Stella turns to face her sister. Side by side they are really a marvel of genetics and rhinoplasty. She says, 'Kiki, you see things exactly as you wish them to be because you're a terrible fantasist.'

'Hey now,' Ryan says.

Stella turns back to her lobster as if she has solved the matter. She slips her wedding ring up over her knuckle and back down again.

The dogs come skittering into the room and squeeze beneath my chair, their limbs rubbing against mine, nuzzling and begging for a morsel of food. I stroke their haunches and they whine a little, waiting for me to give in. Joanna steers the conversation to baby stories of Stella. She cannot resist the nostalgia of her eldest as a child and indulges in a retelling of her first casting in a television advert which we have all heard many times. Kiki gazes at the window even though the drapes are closed. We finish another bottle of wine.

'Frankly,' Stella says abruptly, 'I don't know what we're going to do. I would have liked him here. I would like him by my bloody side for once.'

Everyone stops eating. Our eyes follow as Stella reaches across the table and takes the bottle of Chablis from its silver cooler. Ryan looks away first. The wind hisses through the swollen pane of the window. 'I'll fix that for you in the morning,' he says. 'Little sanding should do it.'

'Angel, what's this all about?' Joanna asks.

Stella lowers her voice until it comes from somewhere deep inside her gut. 'He thinks the kids and I are going to move with him to Qatar for work. I don't want to move to *fucking* Qatar.' The peach tones of her skin darken. Her eyes dart about, the usual decorum spooling like a reel of ribbon.

'Surely you can work something out,' Joanna says with a light laugh. 'You don't want to leave Hampstead.'

Stella glares at her.

I reach for the Chablis, find it empty, fondle the bottle for a moment, and then put it back. In the silence I can hear the wind try to rock the foundations of the house until Kiki clears her throat. 'So, I was thinking, Edie, that you might be my model for life drawing. Not naked, of course, that would be weird. Maybe just exposed shoulders. You have such an interesting face.'

Everyone turns from Stella to me. 'What?' I ask.

Kiki giggles. 'Well, it's not like I could impose a feminine shape on *you*.'

Stella cuts her off. 'No one in this family fucking listens,' she says. 'It's like I'm invisible. You all just do exactly what you bloody well want.'

She storms out, trying to slam the dining-room door behind her, except she can't because the wood has swollen.

Thoroughly drunk now, I murmur, 'Okay,' to Kiki, who claps and raises her glass to mine.

'What's wrong with you both?' Joanna hisses. She follows Stella out of the room.

Ryan finally looks appalled.

But all this is nothing new. Another awkward dinner. A few sharp words. An icy glare. Stella will return in time for dessert, blow out the candles on her birthday cake which only Ryan and I will eat. Joanna will be too involved in her daughter's marital drama to pay any further attention to Kiki and me. We'll cycle back to normal.

My love for Joanna is an old thing, a reliable classic white shirt pulled from the wardrobe time and again. Dressed up, dressed down, it endures countless iterations. Of course, every so often it occurs to me that it cannot be endlessly worn. At some point, the brightness will fade and the stitches which have become loose over time will untether completely. The fabric will not hold its shape unaided. It needs mending, care must be taken.

I wear the shirt and it conceals the aging shape of my body. I wear the shirt and it conceals the nebulous questions I have been ignoring. They've been there for years and I ought to address them but I don't. Or can't. I simply put on the shirt – what a clever shirt – and I leave the house and then I return. But the questions, they do the same. They leave, they return. They will only be ignored for so long. The more I keep them waiting, the more restless they become.

There was a game I played with my friends at primary school. We dared each other to leap between the stepping-stones in our playground – a make-believe river of swirling green water below. I led the group, barked out orders, told the girls to hurry up and stop being sissy. I tucked the edge of my skirt into my waistband and leaped higher and further than anyone else. I always went first. I never thought I would fall. Not even when each of the girls took their own eventual tumble. Scraped knees, snotty tears – that would never be me. I took great pleasure in helping them up, wiping the detritus from grazes. I snuck a look at Clara's navy-blue knickers. I'd watched my father with the women in our block long enough to know how to make girls feel better. I moved just like him. Gentle whispering. Hot breath on small earlobes.

One afternoon, I jumped from our stepping-stones into a puddle and splashed my uniform with mucky autumn water. When I got back to Carlton Mansions, my mother was furious. 'This is not how nice Jewish girls play,' she said.

To deflect, I asked if my father was Jewish, too.

She tutted. 'Of course! What a thing to say. Who have you been talking to?'

'And you, are you Russian? Ukrainian? English?'

'Jewish,' she said quickly. 'And nothing else.'

I pressed for more details about her birthplace – a request she usually ignored. But this time she told of her flight from Odessa with her mother, Sonya, to join her aunt who had secured lodgings in Stamford Hill. They escaped just before the city fell. 'Another pogrom,' she murmured. Not knowing what it meant, I loved the word pogrom and rolled it, silently, in my mouth as she spoke. 'Part of our journey was by boat,' she said, 'and we were at sea for many days. I was so sick. I couldn't stand it. I asked the ocean to take me, but he wouldn't oblige.'

'The ocean or God?'

'But they are the same,' she said.

'And then?'

'And then London. Your great uncle was a doctor in Odessa but could only find work here in a cardboard factory. *Oy*, he toiled and toiled until he had a heart attack two years later. At the funeral, my mother caught the factory owner's eye and they married, reversing her fortunes considerably. He moved us to St John's Wood.'

'Where you met Father.'

'Where I met your father.'

'At a dance,' I prompted.

'Yes, *ziskayt*,' she said, and I knew then all was forgiven with my school uniform. 'Such a handsome Spaniard –

and one who worked at the UN, no less. He fell so deeply in love with me that he converted. That,' she said, pointing a finger towards the roof, 'is the power of love and the power of God.' She sighed. 'But my mother, your grandmother, never spoke to me again. She said I had sullied the bloodline.'

I nestled my head in her lap then, and she stroked my cheeks. I asked her to tell me more, and she lit up as she touched on old wounds, finally letting the stitches unravel and gather at her feet. Half listening, I studied her handsome features, feeling myself part of her orbit, circling closer to her sun. It was here I learned to elevate suffering to the highest form of human bond.

And what about me? What was I? Spanish? British? Jewish?

'My daughter,' she replied. 'You are my daughter.'

It's cold in our bedroom but I open the window, let the night come in. The rain's stopped and the wind has that freshly washed smell. Silver moonlight sneaks through the gaps in the curtains and turns the cream walls murky. In one corner, plaster periodically drifts down from the ceiling. A small pile gathers on the wood floor and flutters in the breeze.

Joanna is sitting on the side of our bed with her back to me, smoothing lotion into her feet. I don't know if the bad mood from dinner has fully dissipated but I go to her anyway, run my fingertips up her spine until it straightens. She's wearing a pink cotton chemise and I slide first one strap, then the other, from her shoulders. She is silent as I kiss a mole somewhere near her spleen. A moan as I slip lower. The crease of her buttock, the right hip bone. Skin smooth, folding in places.

I like Joanna best this way: pliable, wilted, blank – save for the odd gasp. Sometimes it's better between us, without words.

I get to work on the rest of her body. It doesn't take

long. I know all her pleasure zones; my hands move with muscle memory, with rigour. Once I've seen the release in her face, I'm satisfied. She rolls away and soon she's asleep and the night is still again. I peel my breasts from her back, settle into tangled sheets, sweat cooling on my forehead.

In the dark hours, the different women I've had display themselves to me. There is an entire parade of them, longer than my mind can hold, and I shuffle the order to refresh my view. So many gratifying memories, different tastes and smells. Toned, ample, gleaming bodies. Some older, some worn out with pleasure. I think about how fidelity is stupid and wonder how it happened to me.

Click shuffle: the women switch places.

My clit begins to harden again. I slept with many beauties in my prime. Some nights I'll choose just one, beckon her over to the bed and ask her to bend over. Or else I'll gather a group – well balanced, a good mix of shapes – and lie there, passive, letting them crawl over me, hot breath in my ear, stroking the dark hair under my arms, exploring. There's no limit to their curiosity.

Other times, I just want to talk, to fall asleep to the sweetness of a new old voice.

Lust makes anything seem possible the way optimism makes anything seem possible until suddenly one day it's not enough.

'I just don't like that girl,' my mother liked to say about Clara. 'There's something off about her, something not quite kosher.'

Clara and I became best friends the first day of primary school. She lived three streets over and each morning and afternoon we walked to and from classes together. Sometimes we held hands. Clara's father had died when she was two – a tragedy I found deeply desirable for the strange orphan quality it gave her, despite her mother being alive. She was the youngest of six children, the only girl, the spoiled late baby. Her family was boisterous and messy, too many bodies crammed into too small a space. Spills and hollering and always a pot of something bubbling away to nothing on the stove. It made Carlton Mansions seem like a graveyard.

As we grew older, Clara's hair became redder, her cheeks rosier. I was her dark and moody low-voiced friend. Being less popular was no skin off my nose. *I* was her chosen one. I knew everything there was to know about Clara. If there were peas at dinner, she hid them in her socks which were white – always white – with a lace trim. She favoured side plaits over French braids. Her favourite animal was a horse. The thing she loved most in the world was her mother's silk scarf which smelled of dusky roses. I was also the only one who knew how much Clara liked to play doctors and nurses. She had warm hands, sweaty palms. The first time I lifted her shirt, I was surprised to find her nipples as brown and puffy as mine.

By the time we were eleven, I was having trouble looking at Clara. Her amber eyes, their curved fringe of pale lashes. The rounds of her cheeks so plump I longed to pop one into my mouth. I could not bear all that beauty. Her perfection was painful, so severe I felt compelled to be cruel, to pass the pain on, pinching the tender fat of her armpits, pulling the lengths of her silky hair, holding it like a rope in my hands as if I could hang her with her own body. I hurt her in the way I'd learned from my mother: I gave, then took away my affection. Gave, then took it away again.

Clara endured. No retaliation. No complaint. It was like she was immune to pain, accepting her lot. One morning, I elbowed her ribs in the queue for the vault at gymnastics. She made no move but simply turned her eyes heavenward like one of the saints my father used to worship. And, as ever, when afternoon bell rang, she was waiting for me at the gates.

We stopped at her house first. 'The boys are still at work,' she said. 'Ma, too.' She pulled a piece of twine from her blouse, a large key dangling from its end. It was rare for her house to be empty. She smiled. Beyond that pink mouth were teeth as pale as pearls. I had to look away.

In the kitchen, she spread a thick layer of strawberry jam on two slices of white bread and handed one to me before gesturing to her bedroom which she shared with her youngest brothers.

Clara had fashioned a den from old floral sheets, inspired by her mother's stories of woodland sprites, beautiful nymphs and fairies. Mildew lent a mossy smell to the nook. She'd strung Christmas lights inside; they blinked on and off, yellowish white. We crawled into its warm depths, munching in happy silence. The jam and bread became claggy, stuck to the roof of my mouth. Swallowing her last bite, Clara rummaged in a wooden box and pulled out a fake stethoscope. We hadn't played that game in a long time. But instead of me being doctor, and her nurse, she insisted on reversing our usual roles.

A cardigan shrugged off shoulders. A blouse lifted. A heartbeat – mine – hammering away against the plastic.

I closed my eyes as she examined me, let myself untether from the canopy of dank sheets and turn them into interlocking leaves instead. I raised long thin branches over which squirrels scrambled and slices of sunlight patterned the ferns. The air filled with the scent of bluebells, wet soil, the whispered laughter of nymphs.

Before I knew what was happening, there was her mouth – dew-drenched. The taste of overripe fruit sweetened with sugar. She pressed herself against my body. Heat.

Not so much the beginnings of desire, but an arrival so fully formed as to feel it had always been there.

Bleary Saturday morning. Lips smelling of a rose balm, Joanna kisses the side of my face. I inhale the scent, roll over, drift back to sleep.

When I finally open my eyes again, Joanna has gone. The familiar guilt-fear of too much white wine rushes in alongside remnants of a dream where a noxious cloud above my head threatened to burst with sulphur. I knew, in that way you do with dreams, the cloud was my mother. Thirty years I've lived with women but there's still a part of me waiting for my mother's threats to come true, for her to descend, scoop me up and take me to some place terrible where I can be *fixed*. And yet – I wonder about her eightieth birthday, if she'll be able to muster any joy today. Sometimes curiosity can be a betrayal.

I stretch out, plant myself in the middle of the bed. I don't know why Joanna rises so early. We have nothing to rush to. Our days are leisurely. A few chores for me. Exercise classes for Joanna; it's a full-time job to look as good as she does. I have always admired her boundless energy, even for things I do not understand.

When I'm not cleaning, I wander through the hallways, across the grounds, listening to my Walkman. I read the papers. I read erotic novels. I smoke and smoke and smoke. I walk the dogs, pat their haunches. Joanna and I eat together, drink together. We have sex.

I remain grateful to live in this huge house in this beautiful part of the country. England's Garden. Sandy beaches. No traffic sounds. There is so much space here it doesn't matter that the house is crumbling. A wall could collapse and we'd simply walk around it. How different from Carlton Mansions. I would like to tell my mother how I enjoy the solitude, how in many ways I am in control of my time. There's still comfort here even though the gilt has faded. I hear her sharp laugh. *Who are you trying to convince, Edie?*

I pull myself out of bed, wash my face, pad downstairs in a dressing gown to feed the dogs. I brew coffee as they chomp. And then I remember promising to be Kiki's life-drawing model. I hope she has forgotten.

I find Joanna in the conservatory tending to the plants. She angles the green watering can so that a perfect arc streams from its spout. She is inordinately proud of her plants. Morning light floods the glass room. I sip coffee, watching from the hallway. She's wearing workout clothes, sleek Lycra in pistachio with burgundy accents, which follow the outline of her sculpted body.

She turns and jumps when she sees me. 'Darling!'

'You look gorgeous.'

She smiles then, teeth sparkling. 'I'm off to step class,' she says.

'The girls up yet?'

Joanna raises her brows. 'Ryan already dropped Stella at the station. I expect Kiki will emerge around midday. She's going to stay another night.'

'You want some toast before you go?'

She shakes her blonde bob, reminds me to take the dogs out, kisses me goodbye. She leaves a layer of sticky gloss on my bottom lip.

In the kitchen, the dogs have curled up for a post-breakfast snooze. I find Ryan's package in the fridge, blood pooling on a plate. As I unfurl the greaseproof paper, another smaller bundle falls out. I haven't kept kosher for years but bacon still feels forbidden. It's never in the house – too unhealthy for Joanna to request and Harry was more of a beefsteak and fried eggs kind of man. These slices are streaked, flesh and fat marbled. I can feel my mother watching me. *Pork, Edie?* she scolds. *The shellfish wasn't enough?* I try to ignore her but each time I push the voice away it returns stronger, more insistent, like shaved hair that grows back thicker and more wiry than before. 'Fuck it,' I say to the dogs.

I heat oil in a pan, separate the rashers. They pop and spit, curl at the edges. It smells glorious. Rich and salty. I turn them over, expose their brown bellies. There's half a brown loaf in the bread bin and I toast two slices and hunt for the ketchup. I keep it in the fridge but Joanna puts it back in the cupboard. Toast buttered, I press the bacon still dripping onto one side and then smother the other in ketchup. I bite down. The sides ooze. My mother made a lot of bad choices; not eating bacon was one of them.

I take the plate to the velvet banquette and demolish the sandwich. 'It isn't a bad life,' I tell the dogs. I can imagine my mother's response. She would see it as a whispered confession, an admission she was right. She would say I am nothing but an eel following in a stronger specimen's slipstream. That I am a liar, even to myself. I can see her now, lowering her cat's-eye glasses down her nose. *You just tell yourself that,* ziskayt. *Whatever you need to get by.* She would say I'm telling tall stories. In the old language: *Di bobe-mayse.* In turn, I'd recall the response, tell her to suspend disbelief – this is my story now. I'm the one who's telling it.

On Friday afternoons the women of Carlton Mansions came together to eat cake and play Kalooki. I never saw any of the men in the building. They existed only as a talking point.

It was my mother's turn to host that day. Our kitchen had a sash window which opened out onto a ledge protected by an overhang. My mother kept a chicken-wire cage there and would fill it with vegetables that didn't fit in our small fridge. I'd had a bellyache all morning and was supposed to be in bed, but I enjoyed sitting on that ledge, the strange inside-outness of it, my stockinged feet dangling beside the cage. I was there when Vera appeared at the door, clutching a freshly baked *gugelhupf*. Her face was dark and shrewd, eyes looking everywhere at once. She brought with her the smell of cleaning products. A true *baleboste*.

I rested my chin on my knees, hoping I'd go unnoticed and could stay. I loved the kitchen. It was the only room in our home that was not red. How my mother adored that colour, all shades: maroon, pillar box, burgundy.

Curtains, carpet, three-seater sofa, two armchairs, wallpaper and blankets. It lent the flat a ghoulish pink glow which deepened or faded as the sun changed position. But the kitchen had escaped my mother's predilection; it was cream and orange, always sparkling, with a square balcony overlooking Paddington Recreation Ground.

'What are you doing there, Edie, *ziskayt*?' Vera said, turning away from my mother. 'Keeping the vegetables company?'

I couldn't help myself – I jumped up and rushed over to offer my cheek for kisses.

'She's not bashful,' my mother said, disapprovingly.

Margery, Rivka and Dora arrived. I hovered, greeting the women, touching my lips to their powdery skin, inhaling their various scents, hoping to be asked to join them and given a slice of cake. But my mother swatted me away. 'Little girls with bellyaches can't be eating *nashn*.'

My staying home from school was an annoyance and my mother spent the morning ignoring me, consumed by her own torpor, flitting between listlessness and an irritation that clung to her like a membrane. She did not believe I was really sick and she was right – I doted on her and wanted nothing more than to spend the day by her side. My mother's capacity for intensity was intoxicating, her features contorting with the emotion that ripped through her body several times a day. At once playful and tender, in the next moment she was unreachable, locked away behind some private wall. The colder she became, the greater my need to be close. Even when she pushed me away, I enjoyed the sensation of her solid body. My love for her lived in a tangled knot inside my belly. I was sure it was the source of my many stomach aches which disappeared after a morning spent at home.

Vera sat and divided a pack of cards into two piles, making an arch and collapsing them together over and over. The room filled with cigarette smoke. Not only was I not invited, but they'd forgotten about me altogether.

I disappeared from sight like a good girl. Out of sight, but still close. There was a wooden ottoman in the hallway where my parents kept their keys and if I curled up beneath it, I could hear the women talking, see flashes of their faces.

My mother made Camp Coffee, spooning the essence into porcelain mugs, warming milk in a pan. Margery cut the cake and I licked my lips as the sponge crumbled. I'd only been given dry toast and a hard-boiled egg to eat all day. The women began speaking all at once as if they hadn't seen each other in years before quietening down to exchange stories of the week with its recurring theme of injustice. Their voices floated over to me clearly, rising, defending, bleating in their mixed European timbres. The women of Carlton Mansions lived quite literally on top of one another and everyone knew everyone's business. They judged each other terribly and I couldn't tell if they even liked one another. But there was an ease with which they gathered in the kitchen and sat around our table, a natural intimacy I envied but which my mother had already taught me arose from shared horror.

I knew some mothers sang their children to sleep, but mine had taken to spinning bedtime tales of exile and persecution – not her own, but the other women's. I'd once made the mistake of assuming all these women were the same: married Yiddish-speaking homemakers, gossiping card players, whose ties to the old countries only became visible when they baked. But Margery, who worked as a seamstress, had originally come to London as a domestic worker, a *servant*, my mother hissed, before the war, and never offered an opinion, always waited until everyone else spoke. Rivka and Dora were camp survivors – a detail my mother had whispered to me after I'd asked about their tattoos and then never mentioned again. The fright from all those years was still in their bones, my mother explained, and I imagined a kind of sticky marrow accumulating around their joints, pulsating with trapped memories. Their histories were larger than their lives.

If my mother ever told the entirety of her own story to the women of Carlton Mansions, I never heard it. She seemed to prefer complicated anecdotes about insult and malice at the butcher, or how the girl at the cinema ticket booth gave her sass. The women sucked on these stories as if at the teat, gorging on salacious details.

In the cold hallway, I yearned to be not on my mother's lap but by her feet, under the kitchen table, luxuriating like the stray cat Rivka had taken in and doted on.

Vera was sneering about the new arrival on the ground floor. 'An unwed *shiksa*,' she muttered, shaking her head.

'I hear she's throwing a *Christmas* party,' Dora added.

The women became quiet then, and I had to concentrate to catch their conversation. When I heard my mother laugh and say, 'How your family lied to you, promising you'd become a princess in this city,' I left my hiding place and crept closer to the door.

Margery's hands shook as she grasped her cards and spoke her words in a tumble. 'They've never felt I was good enough for my Jacob,' she half whispered, ignoring my mother and directing her comment at Vera. 'I had nothing when we met, no money, no education. But I loved God, oh yes. And there I was in shul every Sabbath and there was Jacob. But in their eyes, I am not religious enough. How they love to make this point, *oy*, over and over. And we're at Friedman's and my father-in-law he calls me a—' She stopped to draw breath and then whispered the word *kike*. 'And Jacob? He does nothing. Nothing.'

Rivka let out a low moan.

Dora was nodding. 'My husband's family is the same. I give him three sons. Three. But still they think I am not worthy. They say they don't understand why other Jews could save themselves and the Polish Jews didn't.'

Rivka let out another moan, this one deeper, more pained. She touched her palm to her forehead. A flash of numbers on flesh.

The other women clucked and shook their heads.

'I try to explain that six million didn't save themselves,' Dora wailed.

'*Ze nakhon*,' Vera said firmly. 'It's true.' She rested her cards face down on the table and closed her eyes for a moment.

Everyone followed suit but my mother, who rearranged her cards and then lay a joker on the pile with a small smile. 'Why did he let it happen?' she said quietly, and then, in a firmer tone, 'Why does he let them treat you that way?'

The other women snapped up their heads.

'He's an animal,' my mother said.

Her comment cut the air. The afternoon light, always warm in the kitchen, grew grey and thin. It wasn't her words that startled me, I was used to this sudden change of mood, but how public it was. She had witnesses beyond me now. And there was a bitterness in her tone I'd not encountered before.

Margery picked up her cards, put them down again.

Even from my hiding place, I could feel the charge between the women. No matter how badly they were treated, they did not speak so bluntly against the men. But my mother did not seem to understand the rules. Compared to the other women, she was in a lucky position. My father doted on her, and his job gave her the freedom that money and time alone could buy.

Vera cleared her throat. 'You go too far, Zelda,' she said, resting her hands on the table, splaying her fingers wide. She was saying, no more, Zelda. Stop.

But my mother did not read the signs, or else she chose to ignore them. 'Jacob's a brute. We all know. Why pretend?'

Margery crumpled.

I, too, made myself smaller, torn between fear and fascination. There was a brilliant relentlessness to my mother's venom.

Only Vera met my mother's force so that they were like two snakes rising from a charmer's basket, twining around each other, tantalisingly close.

'Margery deserves more respect from you,' Vera said.

My mother's lips compressed. They continued to stare at one another.

And then from nowhere – rain. The women turned their heads to the window, watched it lash against the glass. It was the sort of downpour that threatened to harden into hail. Its effect was mesmerising and the room became very still. Their eyes locked, Vera and my mother did not move. The wind raged and shadows played across the walls.

Finally, my mother sighed and went to pull down the sash window, closing the gap where I'd been sitting earlier. Behind her back, the women's expressions twisted horribly. I curled into a tighter ball. I saw it clearly now: my mother was not liked. Like me, they feared her judgemental tone, her unpredictable response to everyday problems. They were aware, much sooner than I, of how she wounded others rather than attend to her own wound.

As if the weather had washed the moment away, one by one the women returned their attention to the card game. Rivka announced she was going to powder her nose.

I jumped up and ran but it was too late. Rivka had

seen me. I scuttled under the ottoman and pressed my back against the wall.

. She knelt down and stretched out her neck until we were level, her round eyes boring into mine. 'I play this game with my puss puss,' she whispered. 'She hides when it's time to clip her claws.'

I said nothing, waiting to be told off for eavesdropping.

But to my surprise Rivka smiled at me. 'Such pretty curls,' she said, extending a thin hand. She stroked my hair gently, lightly.

Her hand moved to the back of my neck. I closed my eyes. She pulled me closer, her hair tickling my thigh. Rivka was frail and the other women teased her about her underdeveloped figure, but they were all jealous of her hair. Pale gold, long and thick, she wore it in a single girlish braid which looped around her shoulder.

'You have your father's skin,' she murmured.

My eyes flicked open.

She giggled. 'Coffee to your mother's cream.'

I felt the observation in my nerve endings.

When the women left, my mother called my name. I didn't reply. I wanted to punish her – first for casting me away, then for the embarrassment of her outburst. I watched how she moved lazily through the flat, her large buttocks filling my view.

'Edie,' she said, her voice all warmth, all honey.

I tried to make my bones and muscles dissolve into nothing.

Finally, she saw me. 'What are you doing down there?' She bent and tried to scoop me into her arms. 'Come closer,' she commanded. When I refused, angry that it was now convenient for me to be her pet, she tutted and gave up, retiring to her bedroom. 'The cake is on the kitchen table,' she called out.

I held my breath. I could have cake. She was sorry for leaving me out. She loved me. I was her *mamele* again.

'Take it down to the bins,' she said. 'Vera cannot bake to save her life.'

The last thing I want this morning is to be looked at. Despite the bacon sandwich, my temples throb, my stomach churns. Kiki stomps around in those awful clogs of hers trying to find the ideal place for her sketch, breathless as she enthuses about her visit to the Turner Prize exhibition last weekend. She went with Chloe, who is also a student at the RA. We've never met Chloe but have been told she is very smart and very serious – a description which makes me feel loyal to Ryan.

Kiki is particularly excited by Tracey Emin's *My Bed*. I read about it in the papers and thought it sounded stupid. I tell her I've had enough post-break-up benders without thinking they could be turned into art. She says I should pay attention to the new wave of women artists, what they have to say about our lives. I groan. But Kiki ploughs on, listing the items Emin arranged around her bed. Crumpled tissues, period-stained clothing, a tampon, cigarette butts, Polaroids, an empty vodka bottle, a pregnancy test, lubricant, condoms. She refers to it as an installation but I don't know what it's installing in anyone apart from the idea that it's okay to make your private mess public and we are *really* not about that in this house.

I trail behind as Kiki enters and exits rooms and tell her it sounds like some kind of solipsistic crime scene.

She shakes her head. 'I can see how the piece might appear static but it's not. The bed is folding, turning, moving,' she says. 'Rolls of sheets like rolls of female flesh. Emin's forcing you to consider the events that led up to her making that mess. It's a true self-portrait.'

'Truth has no business rubbing shoulders with art.'

She looks at me with mirth. 'What do you know about art? Or truth, come to think of it. You're full of secrets.'

I want to snap that it is her mother who has always been secretive but I manage to hold back.

She drops it and focuses her attention on the conservatory. It's a space dominated by one of Harry's hunting paintings: horses and dogs and uniforms. She walks its circumference, head tilted. I imagine she is appraising the light, but the light is grey. With a few exceptions, it's been grey for months. I point out that it's brutally cold in here. She points to the chaise longue.

'You're not serious?'

She nods.

'No one has sat on that thing in a decade.'

'You'll be reclining. Just concentrate on being Rubenesque. Except darker. And butch.'

I look down at my hopelessly straight hips and, only half joking, ask if she's punishing me for something.

But Kiki laughs and says no. I'm doing her a favour.

She is grateful. Ryan has even left me a bag of weed to say thank you.

I smile. Now I can float above this week while Joanna and Stella spend hours on the phone discussing Stella's marital dramas. Joanna insisting how dreadful it would be for Stella to leave her home in Hampstead. Stella retorting with disparaging comments about her mother's choices, never naming me, never needing to.

Kiki pulls the chaise away from the glass doors. It makes a long, protracted sound as it scrapes against the tile floor. She rearranges four damask cushions, plumps them by squeezing their sides, and a small dust cloud appears. She turns back to me, eyebrows raised. Even Kiki still can't shake the notion that I'm The Help. I'm startled for a moment and then shrug. I fetch a portable heater from the kitchen.

I want to know how long it will take – the dogs need walking – but Kiki just tells me to sit back and switch off. 'Imagine being far away from here.'

The idea of being far from here is pleasing. Kiki comes over and I let her twist my body into her desired pose. For a moment I close my eyes but I'm reminded of other times hands have manoeuvred my limbs to form the shape of their desires so I open them again. Kiki slips my top, then bra straps, off my shoulders with the gentle, detached touch of a nurse. Despite the heater, the air is still too cool, too penetrating. She places my elbow on the head of the chaise, cups my hand so that the palm cradles the side of my face. She tries to coax my hair to one side before understanding the curls do no one's bidding.

'Many have tried before you,' I say. 'There's no making pretty here.'

'Who would want to make you pretty?' she asks, genuinely confused. She cannot begin to imagine me as a girl. For the young, the old have always been old. It's inconceivable to her that my mother once forced me into tea dresses and pink ribbons. How she scraped back my hair into some semblance of a bun. How I had to smile for the camera. First day of school. Hanukkah. Bat mitzvah. And now there she is: my mother's spectre hovers behind Kiki, peering over her shoulder. It is my mother's face as I remember it. Proud and lined, the jowls pronounced, full lips painted that Yardley pinkish-red. She lowers her cat's-eye glasses, frowns. *Oy, nothing so interesting about you.* She is a solid presence even when absent. Happy birthday, mother. I haven't forgotten.

Kiki commands me to relax and pushes my shoulders back down. She asks me how it feels and when I reply awkward and unnatural, she says, 'You love attention. Just enjoy this.'

She's right, but I only love attention I can control.

Kiki settles on the couch opposite, a sketchbook on her knees, and pops open a tin of pencils. 'Emin made a mess,' she says, 'but then she chose to get up, get out of it. She redeemed herself, sublimated her shit into art.'

'There were skid stains, too?'

Kiki snorts.

'Don't you think she's crafting her own persona?' I ask. 'Turning her life into a performance?'

'She's taking *control* of her persona,' Kiki says. 'It's different.'

I recall the week Kiki and I spent watching *The Real World* on MTV, shortly after Harry died, when Joanna slept the days away on Valium. Stella had gone to Paris for a modelling job. It was the first time Kiki and I had spent any time alone. We watched TV for hours, buried beneath a blanket, only getting up to pee and refresh our whiskey colas. With all her fancy education, I couldn't believe she was interested in so-called reality TV. But as Kiki caught me up on the domestic dramas of strangers, I found myself enthralled. Confessions aired on prime time, self-discovery in real time. I couldn't look away, allowed the videotape to keep playing. Another one, another one. Eject, flip over, fast-forward the credits, play.

I ask if she remembers when we were obsessed with that programme, how we lost entire days.

Kiki holds her pencil away from her. 'I can't believe that's how we dealt with our grief.'

I swallow, uncertain if I grieved when Harry died. 'Did those people seem real to you?'

She shrugs. 'They're tropes, but I found that comforting. I liked how they orchestrated a narrative. I'm still addicted to reality TV, actually.' She frowns then and instructs me to keep still. All of a sudden, her hand flies across the page. She looks directly at me, not at the paper.

I realise I am shifting my weight forwards. I thought

keeping still might be like keeping quiet but it's not. Sitting in one place, trying to keep my gaze trained on the same spot, my body trembles. I don't think I've ever been looked at with this much care.

'You're blushing,' Kiki says.

I admit I'm a little embarrassed. If my hair has kept its shape and colour, then my face has run away from me. Fleshy pockets, deep lines which stretch from the side of my nose to the corners of my mouth. Joanna, who refuses to age, told me they're called nasolabial folds, more pronounced for some than others. I inherited mine from my mother – the Eastern European countries having a tendency for this particular wrinkle. On the whole, reminders of mortality are thoroughly depressing, but I have a particular affection for the lines on my forehead. They are proof that sometimes I show my displeasure.

We fall silent. There seems to be no precision to Kiki's movements. Just watching her makes me feel loose. I wonder if she's absorbing our conversation into her work. When she frowns and pushes the pencil harder into the page perhaps it's because I've annoyed her, or she is annoyed with herself. When she is too careful, giving me an exacting look, I imagine the lines on the page are awkward. When her arm moves freely, there's an energy there, a slackness which feels playful, like affection. What did she say at dinner last night about the process of painting? *Every choice is a loss.*

'But she didn't win the prize,' I say finally.

'Who?'

'Emin.'

'No.'

'Who did?'

'A man.'

I try not to sigh. Kiki sees Emin's mess as a feminist statement. I see it as luxury. The space and time to really fuck things up. But behind the luxury of expression is sadness – that much is clear to me. I think of what my mother held in her body for so many years before it well and truly broke out.

Kiki starts talking about art again, this time a condemned house cast in concrete by another female artist. She tells of rooms that can't be entered, stairs you can't climb, doors you can't open. Rising rents, local outrage, funding spent and misspent. Intimacy, privacy. The vanished lives of women trapped inside their houses. Does Kiki believe that her generation have been dealt a bad hand? My mother stuck in Carlton Mansions, stuck in her past, was not a performance.

When Kiki takes a breath, I realise I've lost the thread entirely. But it doesn't seem to matter. My place is to listen.

'The light on your skin is beautiful, Edie.'

And like that, it clicks. I feel comfortable. It's as surprising as the shift between having no desire to be touched and becoming aroused. No long, slow burn, it's as fast as a lightbulb flicking on, a goal in a losing game.

'Wait – what are you doing with your mouth now?' She tuts. She tuts just like Joanna.

'My mouth? Nothing.'

'It's all . . . crooked.'

I raise my arm and touch my bottom lip. It feels lip-like.

Kiki lets out a great puff of breath. I've ruined her positioning. 'Don't bloody move,' she says. She puts down her pencil and stomps over, picks up my forearm like she's examining a cut of meat in a butcher and puts in back in place.

When she returns to the sofa she seems lost in thought. 'Emin's bed got a lot of bad press from men,' she says. 'I think men have a hard time with female sensuality when it doesn't include them. When it's just women on their own, feeling their way through their bodies, its processes. Because men understand desire when it's in proximity to them. But female desire by itself? Terrifying.'

I ask who was having sex with Emin in that state. If there were condoms and a pregnancy test by the bed, some man looked at a drunk, sad woman and saw her as fair game.

Kiki confesses she hasn't thought of it that way. I watch as the notion takes hold of her and then deliberate whether it's useful to explain that the best sex I've had was with the most abhorrent people. That it was never based on mutual respect. I have fucked women with no moral backbone and it has been sublime.

'You're more like your mother than you realise,' I say before I can stop myself.

Kiki stares at me, miserable. She closes her sketchbook and tells me she's had enough for the day. I've said the worst thing.

Her clogs click across the tiles.

The dogs scamper into the room and Coco jumps on me, turns and turns, and then settles in my lap. I stroke her fur. She is so faithful.

Kiki has left the sketchbook on the couch. I'm surprised to find there is not one part of me that wants to look at what she's drawn.

'How is she?' my father asked, turning down the kitchen radio.

Always 'she' when we spoke of my mother, always 'her'. He'd returned at noon from a week-long work trip to Barcelona. My mother had yet to emerge from the bedroom.

'Not so good,' I said. 'She's saying that thing again. Over and over.'

My father inclined his head, asked me to scrub the potatoes. His hair was darkest black and so slick with Brylcreem it caught slivers of light like an eel moving beneath water.

At the sink I let water flow over the potatoes, the soil funnelling into brown rivers between my fingers. It was late summer and sweat gathered under my breasts. They were new and small, straining against the dress my mother had insisted I wear for my father's return. I scratched at the rough lace collar.

'What does it mean?' I asked. On her down days, my mother's language shifted to Yiddish.

'*Farshporn zol er oyf shteyn?*' he asked. The words were thick and cottony in his Spanish accent.

I looked up at my father. 'You know how to say it?'

His dark eyes flashed. 'She says it so often. And I know what it means because she says it in English, too. *Why bother getting up alive?*'

I stared at him and then we laughed. This terrible phrase summed up our loved one perfectly.

He took the potatoes from me and began to peel them, the skin slipping easily from the flesh. My father was born in Asturias in the north of Spain, a place I'd never visited but had been told enough stories about to be able to see the peaks of the Cantabrian mountains and rugged coast-line and colourful fishing villages. My parents' birthplaces had the sea in common, but while my mother's ocean was frozen over, my father's dipped and swelled under cool clouds, home to the seafood he loved but which was banned in our kitchen. *Not kosher!* my mother would admonish any time a garlicky prawn snuck its way in. I loved my father's cooking like I loved secrets. Most deli-cious was his tortilla – sweet onions and oozing egg, potato wafer-thin and so tender it felt like butter on the tongue.

'The key,' he was saying, 'is the ratio of egg yolk to whole eggs. I make it with four eggs and five extra yolks. Take that to your grave.'

I slapped a hand on my heart. He lightly pinched my right earlobe. '*Mi hija*,' he said. *My daughter.*

I *was* my father's daughter. We had the same crowded

features fighting for attention on our faces, the same deep olive skin. The only thing I'd yet to mirror were the rows and rows of deep-set lines on his forehead which I attributed solely to the stress of living with my mother.

He sliced the potatoes with quick brutal motions out of sync with his swaying hips, his baritone rising above the staticky music. It was a Bush radio, ivory plastic with a long antenna and tuned to a Spanish station somewhere at the end of the dial. His voice rolled over words I didn't understand. I was locked out of both my parents' languages.

If my love for my mother was twisted and confused, loving my father was pure, straightforward – even if the man himself was not. He adored me, of that I was sure. He helped tame my curls, brushing them through with a wide-toothed comb, rubbing olive oil into their ends. He spoke to me in affectionate, slightly bewildered tones as if I were a prize at a fairground game he'd never expected to win. But there was something else behind his voice, like he was considering what else he might have won if only he'd aimed a little higher. How much of this was to do with me and how much was about my mother, I couldn't figure out. I didn't know what came first: my mother's appetite for tragedy or tragedy itself. More frequently now, my mother spoke to us with a venom that burned like spitting oil from a hot pan. Her reality infused ours. It was dark in there. My father spent more and more time away from the house; I spent more and more time at Clara's. She showed me I could grow beyond my mother and into something else entirely.

'Like this,' he said, holding up a slice of potato. 'See how thin?'

I nodded and did my best to copy his rhythm.

'The heat must be very high,' he said, oiling a pan, 'to seal the outside of the tortilla and keep the inside moist. We'll coax your mother to the table this way.'

I hadn't noticed my mother's complicated relationship with food until Clara came for dinner and asked me why she didn't eat. Now I saw how my mother spent many hours cooking only to watch us consume her meals, a flicker of pride only half hidden by her glasses. On the occasions when she gave in to hunger, she'd wait until she couldn't bear it a second longer and then stand by the kitchen counter spooning too-hot food straight from the pot into her mouth, cheeks puffing as she cooled whatever had settled on her tongue, teeth scraping across the silverware spooning more, more food, until the pot was finished. Appetite unleashed, she'd open and close the kitchen cupboards, huff at whatever she hadn't found there.

The hiss of a beer bottle brought me back into my father's domain. I watched as he assembled the tortilla. It filled the pan, fat and succulent. My father hummed to the radio as he watched it bubbling.

'It's almost ready. Go get your mother.'

I cast my eyes towards their bedroom, made no move. I noticed a single white calla lily in a vase on the table.

'Are you afraid of her?' he asked.

I nodded.

'Me too.' He smiled but it was empty. 'A little fear keeps

a person alert. It's good to be alert. We can thank her for that.'

I was thankful for my mother only when she ignored me.

I knocked on the bedroom door, two, three times before I opened it slowly. There was a lump beneath the summer blanket. The air was thick with heat, damp like a cloud about to burst. I rubbed her shoulder, told her my father was home, that he had made us lunch. She muttered to herself, groggy and uninterested, but after a moment threw off the blanket, rose and smoothed down her crumpled house dress. She paused at the vanity table, ran a brush through her dark hair, dabbed lipstick across puckered lips. Still vain through all that sadness.

When we settled at the table, sunlight cast geometric shapes across her face and for a moment she was unrecognisable, all shadows and angles. For a reason I couldn't fathom, my father turned off the radio. The tortilla was presented on a patterned plate with great flourish. Saliva gathered in the corners of my mouth and I praised the dish, how it bulged with sweet onions. My mother didn't speak until he cut her a slice. 'Leaner, dear,' she said. 'Half that.' She touched the smooth petals of the lily.

We ate in silence but it was so delicious I ignored the tension in the room. When my father saw I'd finished my piece, he cut another without asking. Gooey, it slipped onto the fish knife and then onto my plate. I murmured my delight.

My mother tutted. 'Look at you.'

I stopped chewing and raised my head before swallowing. Her hard eyes were trained on me from behind black frames. She hadn't touched her food.

'Are you going to stop for air?' she asked.

I sat up, straightened my shoulders, jutted out my chin.

'Here you are with all this delicious food,' she said, 'eating like a glutton, slurping, no table manners, nothing ladylike about you and your father *encouraging* you. I don't know who to be more disappointed in. When I think of all the things I didn't have at your age.' She paused, caught her breath and hissed, 'You have everything. You have too much.'

'Enough!' My father stood so suddenly his chair clattered to the floor. He picked up the tortilla plate and threw it into the sink. The motion toppled the vase. My mother let out a wail. The front door banged.

My mother's great chest heaved as she sobbed and murmured, '*Mamzer, mamzer.* Bastard. He has another woman.'

I left the table and went to their bedroom, this time drawing back the curtains to let the sun flood in. I pressed my forehead against the window and looked down at the street below. The glass was hot and uncomfortable; I smelled onion on my breath. Soon enough, my father emerged, and I stared at his rigid back until he rounded the corner of Randolph Avenue and turned into Elgin. A young woman on a bicycle appeared. She pedalled so quickly her white dress puffed out like a cloud around her body. How free she looked. I squeezed my eyes shut and wished for years to fall on my shoulders until I was that woman on that bike, in charge of my own day, pedalling to my next destination. I could feel the breeze in her hair, the slight dampness of her crotch pressed into the warm leather saddle. The bliss of speed. How I longed to be unreachable in adulthood. I grasped my breasts with both hands, closed my fists around the flesh. The image of that life floated and pulsed beneath my eyelids and when I opened them it burned brighter before fading away in flashes. I blinked. The woman had gone. The road was still again.

I pushed my cheekbone harder against the pane, caught the end of a curl in my mouth and wrapped my tongue around it. My father had lasted what – two, three hours before disappearing on one of his walks? How easy it was for him to leave me here with my mother. I wrenched open the window. Children shouted and whooped in the recreation ground behind our block. He'd be gone now for the rest of the afternoon, would return flushed from the weather, still sombre but his rage diminished. When I'd ask where he'd been all afternoon, he would only shrug and reply, 'Walking.'

Each time this happened I imagined him setting off with no clear destination, letting one street turn into the next – so unlike the precise way I watched him handle ingredients, or dress for work. He must have known a completely different city to the one I lived in. My world was Carlton Mansions, the route to school, and the five-minute journey to Clara's house. I knew our street intimately. The entrance to the park, the red phone box at the end of the road, the confectioner's with its bell jars full of sweets and the ancient Polish couple who ran it. Maida Vale station was around the corner and whenever I walked past, winter or summer, a cold wind rushed up from the Underground to blast me. A left turn into Elgin Avenue and there was Ellington's newsagent, the greengrocer, Clark's bakery, West Hampstead Pharmacy, the flower shop and the butcher. My mother's presence loomed large over all these places, was with me even when she was not. I couldn't even conjure an image of my father's world.

In my bedroom much later, I was jolted awake by the rhythmic bang of their headboard. I rolled over to go back to sleep, knowing that, at least for a while, order would be restored in the flat.

Six more months and then he left. I never saw my father again.

As I grew older, he existed for me only in taste memories. Stewed white beans with saffron, crushed tomatoes and raw garlic. The way a perfectly cooked egg yolk oozes across a ceramic plate.

I sit by the phone in the hallway fifteen minutes before Simone will call. It's a cosy set-up – a loveseat under the stairs, small side table with a lamp and a notepad for messages. I doodle a star. Pick at my toenails until Betsey saunters into the hallway, slumps on my feet and soon emits loud puffy snores. 'Sweet girl,' I murmur. I doodle a dog.

I missed most of Simone's childhood but when she turned fourteen, she found me working at Mr Adin's pharmacy in Notting Hill. Samuel had just died and she'd been left alone with our mother. We made a habit of secretly meeting for Sunday lunch when Zelda and Vera took in a matinee at the movies. Our favourite pub was in Primrose Hill. We'd devour roast beef and drink red wine until it was time for her to return to Carlton Mansions, sucking on peppermints, trying to sober up.

I've only seen Simone once in the years since I moved to Damson House. She found my life seedy and compromising and told me so. I couldn't pinpoint when it started, but I'd developed a fear of returning to London, of its pace and frenzy, and so a space had opened up between us. We don't see each other, but we are bound to one another. Maybe this is the best definition of loyalty. No one else knows what it's like to have a mother like ours, one who prefers the comfort of her own interests. As children, if either of us went to her, wanting, she would say, *Add them to the masses of other Jews' prayers.* We don't look alike; we don't sound alike. Our shared bond is our common womb. Our common wound: the pain of our mother.

The phone rings. The dog stirs, raises her head, but I don't want my sister to know I wait by the phone so I don't pick up until the seventh ring.

'Hello, Sissy,' I say, leaning back and twirling the cord between my fingers.

My sister greets me. Her voice is so eloquent, so considered. Like our mother, she had elocution lessons although hers were in order to be accepted into secretarial college.

Joanna is always at a Pilates class on Sunday mornings, which means I have space to say whatever I want, but when the opportunity arises, I find I have nothing whatsoever to talk about. So today, like most days, our conversation starts slow and stupid. I ask after her health. She tells me she's still sick but better. She moves on to her week at work as a paralegal, her ten-year-old daughter, Anais, her aerobics classes – like I don't get enough of that with Joanna. She talks about her husband, even though I can hear he is in the room. In return, I spin stories about the dogs, about Stella's birthday, about the lobsters we bought from local shores, how *great* the seafood is here, and then when I run out of things I'm happy to share, I begin to lie. I suppose it should be worrying how easily it comes to me. I make up stories about the neighbours, about a cocktail party. Stuff I know Simone will relate to. I make it easy for her.

In exchange she humours me by asking questions she doesn't want the answers to and in this way we are complicit, both avoiding the topic of our mother which comes, invariably, halfway into any call.

Simone is diplomatic. She doesn't want to upset me so she waits for me to ask and I try to hold out but soon the words *and how was her birthday?* escape my mouth. I attempt to imagine my mother at eighty, face and tits sagging, but no, she remains in her forties – solid and forbidding.

There is quiet at the end of the line and then an intake of breath.

'That good?' I joke.

Simone's earrings clank against the mouthpiece as she shakes her head. 'She's furious with me. Apparently, I didn't make enough of an effort.'

Despite still recovering from the flu, my sister drove to Maida Vale to bring our mother back to her home in Finsbury Park, and then ordered a huge Chinese feast for dinner – our mother's favourite food which, according to Simone, she eats in abundance at any given opportunity. She filled the kitchen with flowers and set out the wedding china. 'At the end of the evening, Mum asked me what she'd done to deserve such a lazy daughter,' Simone says. 'Not cooking for her myself was proof I didn't love her.'

Now it's my turn to be silent, oscillating between guilt and envy. Simone has been dealt a shit hand having to cope with our mother alone. But at least she has had a mother beyond childhood.

'When we said goodbye,' Simone says, 'she wished me a good life. I tried calling her when I got home and again this morning but she just lets it ring out.'

'Sounds like Hanukkah year before last,' I say. 'Remember that? She got over it within a week.'

My sister snorts. I can feel her raise her eyebrows. I've missed the point. 'She talks about death all the time. Her hypochondria's getting worse.'

I don't believe that's possible but I say nothing. My sister wasn't around in the dark years, in the months when my father finally lost his patience, before Simone's father, Samuel, arrived on the scene and saw something in her the rest of us couldn't.

As Simone changes the subject, the many sadnesses of my mother return to me. Days and days in bed. The red walls of her bedroom blackened by drawn curtains. I have never understood why a mother would want her daughter to be sad, to be adrift and displaced as she once was. In the years where I attempted to forgive her, I tried to find power in how she approached life, in the microscopic way she experienced it, the narrowing down, the honing in on a singular feeling, examining it, analysing it, revering it, and then becoming it – wholly. Holy. I tried to see her as conquering some aspect of life – not becoming diminished by it. Now I can see there was nothing powerful about her depression. Her pain went back to her own mother, Sonya, who cast her out when she married my father and of whom I know almost nothing, and to Odessa, where her life had started. She returned to the past to acknowledge the source, not to heal. She felt at home in a long legacy of agony and persecution and displacement. One link of the chain, she was desperate to be heard. Hell, she even shackled me to the chain herself. *Pass it along*, I can hear her mutter. *Pass it along.*

At this point, the knowing of my mother stops. The rest is imagined or coloured in from the small sketches Simone provides. If she had been a good mother, perhaps I would have been a good daughter. It was not my job to pay it back.

I only realise the call has ended and I've hung up the phone when the sound of clogs echoes in the hallway and there is Kiki, her face all sheepish, all sweet. She's wearing a PJ Harvey T-shirt and jeans impossibly low on the hips, a glimpse of orange knickers.

'I've been looking at my sketch of you,' she says, 'and I'm on to something. I can feel it. Can we try again? I go back to London later.'

I want to erase the image of my mother's disappointment, cool the burn of her birthday fury. Speaking with Simone makes it all still too tangible.

I say yes.

In the year after my father left, my mother hid herself away. She rose late in the mornings, ate, had a bath and then went back to bed. Sometimes the order changed. Sometimes she didn't eat. Sometimes she drifted from room to room, ignoring me, all her burning qualities dampened.

One evening, I found her in a bath filled to the edges. A few droplets of water ran down the sides. While my mother was in there, soaking, sulking, I'd returned from school, lit the fire, hammered the chicken to make schnitzel, peeled and boiled potatoes, completed my home-work and called Clara from the payphone at the end of our road.

When I couldn't stave off hunger any longer, I decided enough was enough and went to raise my mother from her watery tomb. She barely noticed when I pushed open the door and balked at the wave of steamy air. Our bath-room was always full of steam, bleeding into the rest of the flat until all was vapour and fog.

I knelt on the bathmat and whispered her name. Not

Zelda, not mother, but *muter*, reaching out with Yiddish, silently hoping she'd reply with *mamele*, little mother, my daughter.

She didn't respond.

The tips of her breasts and her head were all that floated above the soapy water. I asked her to sit up – there was no modesty left. In the movement a fat silvery scar running vertically down her abdomen caught the light. I swallowed down a gasp of surprise. I had no idea I'd been cut from my mother's womb. I fought the urge to wedge my thumbnail in the scar's seam, to peel it open like a piece of fruit.

I set about rinsing the suds from her half-washed hair. There were small bald patches where she'd torn at the strands. She let out a low sound as I smoothed conditioner into the ends. 'There we go,' I murmured. 'That feels better, doesn't it. Now, let's stand.'

I fetched a maroon towel from the stack I'd laundered and placed it around her shoulders. The water was getting cold.

My mother didn't move.

'Time to get up,' I repeated.

'I can't. I can't walk,' she said, her voice loose and miserable. 'There are pebbles. Pebbles in my shoes. I can't shake them out.'

I stared at her murky expression, longing to leave her languishing in the bath, to walk out of the flat entirely. 'What do you mean?'

'The pebbles from the port. They got into my shoes. It's hard to walk.'

Since my father had left, my mother's solid body had been expanding. She ate all the foods she'd always denied herself and I thought this was the reason she'd been walking more slowly, her small feet adjusting to new weight. I shared none of my mother's anxiety about her size, preferred her shapely frame and told her so. But now I realised her gait was exactly like a person coming in from the beach with pebbles stuck in their shoes.

I slipped my hands under her armpits and raised her from the water, wrapping the towel around her body. 'Dry off,' I murmured.

I might not have known what to do with her pain, but I was reasonable. I thought about all that had been taken from her. By marrying my father, she had lost her mother – her only connection to Odessa. Not even her accent had survived intact since Salvatore paid for the elocution lessons that softened her vowels. Now you'd have to be looking for it to catch a glimpse of her home country. If my mother felt stranded at sea, then she had every right to feel that way. He had left us adrift.

I busied myself with dinner as she dressed, trying to mimic the carefree dance my father had conducted with the stove, the oven, the chopping board. I didn't dare break the quiet of the flat with the radio.

I mashed potato with milk and butter while the schnitzel sizzled in a cast-iron pan. The smell of fried, breaded meat rose into the air and soon my mother appeared in her red housecoat. She sat at the table and I poured her a glass of grape juice and set down a plate of food. There were no clean knives, so I stuck two dirty ones under the tap and polished them quickly with a dishcloth. Her eyes were glazed, fixed on another time.

My mother lowered her head and sniffed the plate. 'This looks good.' She sliced into the schnitzel. It was crisp and golden. I'd followed one of my father's recipes – a detail she didn't need to know.

'I suppose you'll be wanting some conversation,' she said. 'Well, Vera got a dog. A brown cocker spaniel.'

'She did?'

'Guess what she called it.'

'Dov?' I joked, naming Vera's husband.

My mother's brows shot up and for a minute I thought I'd pushed her sense of humour too far, but then she roared with laughter.

Wiping tears from her eyes, she said, 'Stinker. She called him Stinker! But I'm going to suggest she reconsider.'

I smiled but we both knew Vera wasn't speaking to my mother. She would have heard about the dog from Rivka, the only one of her old friends who could still tolerate her company and hadn't taken Vera's side. A few months ago, Dov had gone away on a business trip and never returned. The women of Carlton Mansions grew suspicious. They assumed he had another woman somewhere and gossiped behind Vera's back. Rather than extending some kindness, primed as my mother was to understand her predicament, she instead made some quip to Vera no one would repeat to me. My mind thrilled with the possible arrangements of words. I knew I should be embarrassed, but secretly I was proud of my mother's shocking relationship with language – especially when it wasn't directed at me. She was cruel but she was fearless. The truth about Dov, however, was juicier than anything she could have conjured up herself. A scuffle over a hand of cards had soured. He was serving ten years in prison.

It felt like the women of Carlton Mansions were fated to be alone and I was determined not to join their ranks. I fucked Clara at every opportunity. Pressed against the wall in the school toilets. In the gymnasium changing rooms after everyone had gone home. In the warmth of her bedroom den, an old trunk dragged across the door for safety. My fingers were always slick. I could not get enough of her skin, her gasps, her shaking legs, the feeling of being innately intertwined. I would wake each morning still tangled in dreams, the taste of condensed milk in my mouth. Only once did Clara ask if what we were doing was bad. I had no answer. The thought had never occurred to me. Clara had unlocked something I wasn't going to deny again.

'Vera,' my mother said, chomping her schnitzel. '*Makhasheyfe.*'

Poor Vera. She was not a witch; she was a woman abandoned. Just like my mother. But unlike my mother, Vera swallowed her pride and went out to work. The rest of the women continued as usual, cleaned and cooked and cleaned and waited for the men to come through the door, say hello, kiss cheeks, food on plate and beers poured. My mother did nothing. She did less than nothing. She festered and she disappeared into her past.

'*Makhasheyfe*,' I repeated.

She nodded, eyes glinting.

Lately, Yiddish curses dropped from my mother's mouth like globs of poisoned honey. Her syllables were hard and so lyrical they would be beautiful if it weren't for the consternation that accompanied them. I listened to her insults more carefully now, determined to understand the ghost I lived with. I wrote the phrases in my notebook phonetically and practised the sounds.

'What does *hamoves tokhter* mean?' I asked.

'What?'

'*Hamoves tokhter.* You said it the other day. *Khasene hobn zol er mit di malekh hamoves tokhter.*'

My mother snorted and then let out a gust of laughter. 'Oh, that,' she said. 'Very good, *ziskayt.* It is what I think of your father and whoever is in his bed. *He should marry the daughter of the Angel of Death.*'

She laughed again, but her mirth was momentary. 'If only the Angel of Death would be so merciful as to visit me. But no, she is too busy with your father.'

I kicked myself. I'd opened the wound. Her lament didn't even make sense. Wasn't it the Angel's daughter he was supposedly rolling around with?

My mother devoured the rest of her meal and, mouth full, embarked on a sequence of complaints. She'd been having terrible nightmares, darkness on darkness, sending her great body thrashing and writhing through the night. For so long there had been no stories of my mother's early life in Odessa and now, suddenly, a list of dead relatives, blood staining earth. I watched, helpless and horrified, as she tunnelled inside her own sadness. She talked faster and faster, sentences tumbling over one another. She escaped the pogroms in Odessa so she could live. But it seemed that living was not for her. She thought she'd upset God by thwarting his plan and so turned towards the idea of death, opening her arms, taunting it with her willingness to reverse the past, to say, *It was my time. I shouldn't have slipped from your grasp.*

While my mother courted Death, the bills were piling up. They lay, unopened, on the hallway ottoman. I was sure my father had left us something, or else was sending money each month. I didn't dare ask. I'd received just one letter after he'd packed his bags and then, nothing. I hadn't opened the letter. He did not have my forgiveness. I guessed my mother and I had more in common than I liked to admit.

I realised I was being shouted at. 'Sit up straight. Are you even listening?' my mother was saying. 'How am I ever going to find a decent man to take you when you refuse to master basic manners? And what is going on with your shirt?'

My stomach twisted. If only I could tell my mother that she needn't worry about finding me a man. I fixed my stare on a fleck of mashed potato above her top lip. Who was she to talk about manners? There was always something wrong with my appearance. Nothing she wanted me to wear looked right on my body. Everything hung shapelessly from my shoulders, the waist in the wrong place. She wanted to tweak me, like all it would take to conjure the perfect daughter was to re-do a hem or cinch some fabric.

'It's not as if your brains are going to help.' She was flaming now, gathering momentum. How quickly threat rode into the room. 'You're going to need a good husband or else you'll starve. I can only look after you for so long. You stomp around the flat so maudlin. I can't stand to see your unbrushed hair. I can't stand it!'

A year or so earlier I may have felt my heart pounding unbearably at these words. But now I stifled a laugh and remained silent as her voice soared, composing a list in my head of all the things my mother was not. Doting. Affectionate. Interested. Kind. Thoughtful. Helpful. There was no nourishment here. It would have to come from the recipes I'd siphoned from my father – his only legacy stews and soups, fried fish, warm rice pudding with cinnamon apricots. If my mother found me lacking as a daughter, she herself was more like a murder of crows than a mother.

'To think you came from my body,' she said.

'You have a scar,' I said quietly. 'I've not seen it before.'

'They ripped you out! They cut me open and wrenched you from me. You were suffocating, that little neck squeezed by the cord. They ripped you out and ever since it has been me who has been suffocating. I took your place.' She took a breath. 'When did I agree to carry your burdens as if they are greater than my own?'

She waited for an answer.

'Go on, laugh at me. Laugh. I don't care.' Her voice had lowered. She was glowering now. 'Vera knew before I did that I was pregnant with you. You would have been just a speck of sand in my womb when she said, "Zelda, you are with child. What's more, it's a girl." I asked her how she knew and she replied, "There is an adage in the old country. You can tell if the baby is a boy because the mother's face stays pretty during her pregnancy. But if it's a girl, the mother turns ugly, all her beauty siphoned for her daughter."'

Her eyes flashed. 'But now look at both of us. Ugly as each other.'

'It's the hands,' Kiki says. 'I can't get them right.'

Down goes the pencil. Fingers worry through her yellow hair, which is missing its layer of gel today. Without it, the strands are limp and curious, falling in curtains over her forehead. In T-shirt and jeans, she's more androgynous than usual. It's lovely.

Kiki's arranged me in the same pose as yesterday, remembering the way each part of my body folds. But what is it she cannot get right about my hands? Does she see some deficiency in their form? It is true there are so many things my hands have not done. They have not held babies, spooned mush into hungry mouths. They have not been worked raw, or become blistered from wind and sea as my mother's did on her journey to England. Instead, they have navigated the knot of oysters, swirled unpronounceable wines. They have doled out medicine but they have not soothed anyone's brow. They have been idle or else they've been the tools of pleasure – for myself, for others, dextrous and searching and knowing all at once. They have given that way.

And then I find I have been saying all of this to Kiki. I always speak too much or not enough, never getting the balance right. I sigh. 'Your mother would have been a better model.'

At that Kiki laughs and starts sketching again, her pencil flying, looking at me concentrated, squinty-eyed. The heater whirs away at my feet. Rain tips against the conservatory skylight.

'You don't sound yourself today,' she says finally.

'And how is that?'

'Quiet. You're usually quiet.'

I grimace.

'What's on your mind?' she asks.

I am, despite my nonchalance on the phone, deeply disturbed by my mother's treatment of Simone. She is right to be worried. Our mother's most cherished pastime is complaining, *kvetching* as she'd say, though it is darker than that word implies. And for complaining to happen there must be an audience. She loves to tell anyone who'll listen how she suffers, how cruel this world has been. No one more than her doctor who she frequently calls despite disagreeing with any of his diagnosis. *He thinks he's a* gansa macher, *a real man about town,* she used to say. *But really he's just a* schmuck. *Same prescription no matter the problem. What a quack.* My sister's daily phone calls are a lifeline. All that rage must find somewhere to go.

'You can talk to me,' Kiki says.

'I'd rather listen.' It's a phrase which comes to me easily. I prefer to listen and I prefer to watch. How else could I have been with so many beautiful women, especially one as beautiful as Joanna. You cannot fake true attention. It is the one thing I know how to give. There is a particular way of watching women so that they blossom, not shrink. Perhaps this is my life's work, worthy or not.

Instead of pushing me, Kiki launches into a description of another artist she admires. She picks up her pencil again. 'Her short film has been haunting me.'

I ask her to elaborate.

The artist is Naomi Uman, she tells me. *Removed* is a series of scenes cut from a reel of 70s German soft-core porn. Uman doctored the surface of the tape with bleach and nail varnish to extract the women's bodies from the scene but leave the rest intact. 'You can hear orgasmic moaning,' Kiki says, 'and shouts of *Oh yes! Go on!* but where there used to be a woman's body is now a crackling, shimmering white ghost. The men still observe it, still caress it. The women are there but not there.'

I nod.

'But they're not completely erased,' she adds quickly. 'You still search to see the women, to find some kind of narrative, but it's a new way of looking, totally devoid of the kind of desire usually associated with porn. The women escape their passive roles, make fools of the men who grasp and grope at nothing.' She grins. 'I read that Uman described those new crackling forms as animated holes.'

'Animated holes?'

'The invisible made visible again,' Kiki concludes.

I smile and Kiki tells me off for changing expressions.

If I don't apologise it is simply because I want to stay in the embrace of Kiki's enthusiasm, her youthful appetite for change, for wonder. I conjure an image of the video she described. The acid colours of the 70s, the fuzzy quality to the film, the men's thick moustaches, the curvaceous shape of the women's bodies – all familiar to me. I string the scenes together and animate them with my own sense of being present and absent simultaneously. But I'm not comfortable with the suggestion that porn reduces women to a passive role.

When I say so, Kiki shrugs. 'Maybe it's different if you're only watching women on women,' she says. 'But it's always a man behind the camera. You have to remember that.' Suddenly stirred, her pencil darts about the page like a child playing hopscotch. 'The original German porno Uman used is badly dubbed,' she says. 'There's a delay between the moving mouth of the actor and an over-the-top American voice. It's good to see the men become the performance.' She stops sketching and looks at me more squarely now. 'You're moving again.'

I vow to stay still, to be a good model. I focus my mind on what might lie beyond my head and out through the glass doors of the conservatory. The garden bustling. Wind swirling. A bird alighting on a branch then fluttering away. Crocus bulbs turning in the soil, worms weaving around them. A squirrel gambolling across the lawn. A world away from my static body.

'Open your eyes, Edie,' Kiki says.

Her expression is kind. When I agreed to be drawn, I

imagined her classical training at the Royal Academy would lead to a painting with broad, impressionist strokes. But the more she talks, the more I can see how her interests might transform the image of my body. I ask her why she wants to paint rather than explore more modern mediums.

She gives me a hard look before replying that her interests are her interests – not her practice. She doesn't want to follow a fad. She wants to find her own way. She doesn't want it to be all about commerce.

This is not something she could ever admit to Joanna, who turns electric at the feel of crisp sterling notes. But then Kiki doesn't need to worry about cash. She doesn't even need to work. If none of her paintings sold it wouldn't matter a bit. There is a small trust fund, one for her and one for Stella. Harry gambled away the rest of the family fortune and the amount left to Joanna was much smaller than she'd anticipated. It was a last, strangled laugh from beyond the grave. *You cannot have it all.*

Soon, Kiki announces she's done all she can. An hour's passed. I uncoil slowly, like a snake emerging from a woven basket.

She packs away her pencils and then comes to where I'm still stretching. She bends and kisses my left cheek. 'You really are quite exquisite, Edie,' she says into my ear.

I pull back, stunned. It has been so long since someone paid me a compliment. A sudden craving pulls at my belly. After sitting still for so long, my body feels as if lead weights are attached to all my limbs. I'm desperate to float in the air. 'What time's your train back to the city?' I ask.

'I'll drop you at the station if you'll come with me to BounceOut?'

'What?' Kiki laughs. 'The trampoline room at the gym?'

I nod. She laughs again but I'm serious. I explain I took Stella's kids when they came to stay. It looked so fun but I couldn't join in. 'Let's release our inner children?'

'You're fucking crazy,' she says, and then, 'Gimme five minutes to pack my bag.'

In the car, Kiki winds down her window and the rainy afternoon swirls in and whips her hair. We're driving away from the sea, but the air still has its crust of salt. Kiki has found one of my Carly Simon tapes and is singing along to an early song. She knows all the lyrics, which means I am old, *really* old, my youth gone out of fashion and returned again.

Kiki puts her feet up on the dashboard. I speed through the suburbs like I can outwit the grey skies and the grey buildings, turn onto the A-road and hit the gas harder, watching the dial rise until it reaches sixty. Kiki howls along to the music like a wild thing, rain in her hair now.

Suddenly she turns the music down and asks, 'Did Mummy come with you? To the trampoline place? It doesn't seem very . . . Joanna.'

'No,' I say. 'I was sent as a chaperone for Stella's girls. Your sister wasn't very interested in keeping an eye on them.'

'She prefers to pay people for that.'

'I won't hold my breath for a cheque.'

Kiki turns the music off. Wind rattles the car.

'Do you mind, Edie?' she says quietly.

I exit the dual carriageway. 'Mind?'

'How she treats you. Stella, I mean. Well, and Mummy. It's . . . outrageous sometimes.'

My surprise emerges as a deep hacking cough and Kiki tells me that Joanna's second-hand smoke is to blame since I gave up after Harry died. I take deep breaths and somehow manage not to crash the car and in that time, Kiki decides to relieve me of her question. She moves on to talking about Ryan and Chloe, how she's going to have to make a choice soon as they're both getting too serious about her, and I hold it in, how her mother never made the choice, how her mother decided she was going to have everything she wanted, and before I know it we arrive at BounceOut and Kiki is grinning again, swinging her feet like a child. I park, badly, and we ping our seatbelts simultaneously.

Kiki takes my hand, dragging me along, and I briefly get the sense of what it must feel like to be a mother, to find joy in someone younger, purer, bubbling away beside you. I'm surprised I've never felt this before. I'm surprised I can still surprise myself.

When we enter, the teenage attendant gives us a strange look but since it's Sunday and the place is teeming with youths and screaming children, toddlers appearing and then disappearing like rolling waves in a pool of coloured balls, he takes our money and our shoes and points the way to the sports hall.

The room is one giant trampoline, divided into smaller ones by angled edges which make a maze of bouncing rooms. Kiki's eyes widen. 'This place is wild,' she murmurs, taking in the black walls and lime green racing stripes. It smells of feet.

It's so noisy that part of me wants to turn around and walk back out but Kiki is animated, giggling, already climbing onto a corner of trampoline not dominated by ten-year-olds. 'Don't be chicken now!' she yells, finding her footing. And then she bends her knees and bounces into the air. A huge belly laugh erupts from her open mouth and I scramble up to join her. When I struggle to find my balance, she takes both my hands and, grinning, counts, 'One, two, three.'

We launch and then I'm laughing too, tickled by the sudden weightlessness. I break away from Kiki and bounce again. To my surprise, I don't fall straight on my backside. It's like my body knows what to do, like it's been waiting all its life to defy gravity. I bounce and bounce and as I do, Kiki's words rattle in my skull, jangling and reforming.

Do I mind how Joanna treats me?

Do I mind Joanna?

Does Joanna treat me?

Joanna put an end to my money worries. But I'm not sure this is the only way to treat a person. What of the wives who come home with love tokens for their spouses? Not items of worth, but ones of more intimate value. Not once has Joanna brought me a small bag of the chocolate Brazil nuts I like to munch on during the day. Or a new bar of lavender soap – the scent of which she hates but knows I love. There's much to be said for small moments of care.

Up in the air, I'm pleasantly breathless and when I close my eyes for a moment, all the Edies I have been over nearly five decades emerge and show themselves to me.

Do I mind?

For the first time in a long time, I look beyond the present day and consider mine and Joanna's future. Two old, still-vain ladies clattering around an enormous house, trying to keep up with the dogs. New beginnings do exist. Even my mother managed one.

Bounce. *Do I mind?* Bounce. *Do I mind?* Bounce. *Do I?*

The room becomes a blur. Smears of colour. My splintered selves collide with one another, their choreography intricate, elaborate. I push down hard, making my weight work with gravity this time, down down, and when the soles of my feet settle on the trampoline's tight skin, I push and push to spring back up and turn my body mid-air, somersaulting, reaching out my arms to grab at the breeze-block ceiling which appears to me now as a floor. I turn and right myself again and bounce from my bum back to my feet, laughing my head off.

I have never been able to resist the opportunity to try something new. From the innocuous, like trampolining or an obscure delicacy, to more dangerous options like women. Especially women. I have grown to admire strong wills and, despite myself, I developed a willingness to be led. It began with Clara, who liked to make the first move and then push to see if there was a line I wouldn't cross (there wasn't). Then came my first proper girlfriend, Lyra, then a host of beautiful women, each one richer than the last, each one offering me an insight into a way of living I had not known possible. Fate put me in their path. My hand was always outstretched to follow and the strong-willed were always looking for an accomplice; someone to validate their whims. I had no trouble acquiescing, I never thought anyone could do me harm. Inside, there was still that little girl jumping over stepping-stones in the playground, certain I'd never be the one to fall.

If only I had known then how firsts set a precedent, set in motion a pattern you don't know you are forming, one that will replicate itself endlessly and become so much a part of your personality you no longer know who you are without it.

Of course, the strongest will of all was my mother's, who did not bend or break for anyone, not even when she professed to be dying. And then I hear her voice, goading me. *See what happens when you go against God, Edie?* she says. *He comes for you. See how he gets you good.*

Two years after my father left, my mother married Samuel.

They met at a showing of *Swiss Family Robinson*. I knew this because my mother had become secretive, evasive, so I'd taken to reading her diary. It wasn't hard to find. Smooth black leather hidden beneath her knickers in the bedside drawer. Her handwriting was poor; she'd never learned cursive and as a result her letters looked like a child's. To my disappointment, I found nothing salacious. The entries were simple: birthdays, numerous doctor's appointments, engagements, her running tab at the grocer's and kosher butcher's. She gave every film she saw a score out of ten. I don't know what made her the expert.

Samuel was a watchmaker and a Good Jewish Man from Belgium who'd settled in London with his brothers after serving in the navy during the war. Several years my mother's junior, he was so sanguine and composed even my mother couldn't stamp out his light. He took her to the pictures, to dinner, on a pedalo across the Serpentine in Hyde Park. Apparently, it was enough.

In love again, she was transformed. Vibrant and

amenable with a wicked sense of humour. She reclaimed the kitchen. Borscht, chicken and prune tzimmes, salty minced fish. A game of bridge in the evenings. Marrying Samuel meant she did not have to find a job. What mercy – I could not imagine my mother working. She did no one's bidding. Had no sense of time or decorum. Most of her life's pleasure, I suspected, was derived from it being easier than Vera's, easier than the lives of all the other women in Carlton Mansions, each of whom were facing their own particular disappointments with men. Samuel took the spotlight away from my shortcomings and he was good to me. For a while, life at home was bearable.

Soon, Simone arrived. Howling, screaming, but oh how I loved her! The round, blinking eyes. The rolls of fat on her thighs. I kissed and kissed her sweet flesh – pale as her two parents. When we went out as a family, my mother joked that I looked like the help.

As if we had enough money for a nanny.

A few weeks after Simone was born, a new tenant moved into Clara's building. At first, we didn't know what we were looking at. Greying hair clipped short with a severe side-parting. Inky suits, silk ties, starched shirts, tweed waistcoats, thick woollen socks and high-shine pointy shoes. Recognisably female and yet not what we recognised as female at all.

Clara's mother was horrified, wouldn't tolerate a word about her. But the two of us were captivated – a vibrancy about this stranger we couldn't name. We loitered in the corridor for a glimpse when she returned from work, her clothes pristine but dirt under her short nails and smears of something oily on her cheeks. Most days, she carried a paper parcel from the butchers, blood weeping in its corners. We'd say *good evening* and she'd nod solemnly before sliding her key into the door.

Clara and I were slouching around in the corridor playing gin rummy the evening she finally came to talk with us. Her name was Cynthia, she said, but told us to call her Syd. She worked as a mechanic at a garage down the road. I didn't know women could still have jobs like that after the war. We bombarded her with questions about her appearance. Syd laughed. She told us she went to a barber in Kilburn and shopped at the men's department in Fenwick of Bond Street. 'Not often, mind,' she added. 'Things cost a pretty penny.'

'They don't bother you in there?' I asked. I couldn't believe she had the gumption to walk in, let alone be served, try on clothes and hand over money.

'Mostly no.' She smiled a little. 'They're too confused.'

I couldn't tell if she was proud or embarrassed.

I told her I wished I had a suit like hers. All I wanted to do was wear trousers but they were forbidden to me. I could feel Clara staring at the side of my face as I yabbered on. I knew she much preferred dresses and skirts, loved to groom her long red hair, to shape her dainty nails. And she much preferred to be the one doing the talking.

Syd's eyes darted along the corridor, wary of who might be watching. 'This steak won't cook itself,' she said, shrugging and inviting us inside.

Clara and I looked at each other.

Syd unlocked the door and we meekly followed, all bluster disappearing as we shifted from our domain in the corridor to Syd's world.

Her flat was a similar layout to Clara's but half the size. We passed a tiny kitchen and bathroom and entered the living space, which was sparsely decorated. What little furniture Syd had was dark and Victorian. The walls were mustard-coloured, browning where there was damp, and two small oil paintings of landscapes were propped against the mantle above the fireplace. Stale ashtrays bulged with the ends of roll-up cigarettes. There was a sour smell. It was exactly how I imagined a gentleman's study. Syd disappeared into the kitchen.

'See if you can try on some of her clothes,' Clara whispered. I couldn't be so bold, but I deeply wanted to touch every item of clothing, open all the cupboards, examine each can and box of food, rifle through medicines and lotions in the bathroom. Clara slipped an arm around my waist, squeezed hard. I wriggled away. She spoke on my behalf in school, planned what we'd do at the weekend without consulting me. I was tired of it.

The hiss of beer bottles opening came from the kitchen.

'Syd,' Clara called out. 'Could we take a gander in your wardrobe?'

I jabbed a finger into her belly.

'Don't be a wet rag,' she hissed.

Syd emerged and handed us each a bottle of brown ale. I sniffed the top. It smelled like sweet bread. I wrinkled my nose, but Syd laughed, said it would put hairs on my chest.

'You can look in the wardrobe if you like,' she added, gesturing to a door across the narrow hallway.

I blinked hard. Clara thanked Syd, grabbed my hand and strode into the bedroom. She felt along the wall for a light switch and flicked it, casting weak yellow light on a tiny room. There was a single bed pushed into a corner, a pile of books beside it. A chest and two dark wardrobes dominated the space. Clara flung open the doors. 'Edie,' she breathed. I joined her and stared at the rail. Neat rows of blazers, pressed trousers, and shirts so pristine I could smell the starch. I took a sip of stout, swallowing down its acrid flavour. I touched the fabrics gently, with reverence. Clara took out a dark blue blazer and held it against my body.

'Far too big,' she said sadly.

'Slip it on.' We turned to see Syd watching us. 'It's okay. Try it.'

Clara draped the blazer over my shoulders. I set the beer on the floor and then wriggled my arms into the sleeves. There was a mirror fixed to the inside of the wardrobe door and I turned to face my reflection as Clara pulled my hair away from my forehead. The sight disturbed me. Not a girl, not a woman, not a man.

Syd handed me a book from the pile by her bed.

I felt Clara bristle at the attention I was receiving. She was used to being the favoured one. I turned the book over in my hands. *The Well of Loneliness*. The cover showed two ladies in smart, outdated outfits and hats. Syd asked us how old we were, then narrowed her eyes when we said fifteen. She took a sip of ale and when she began talking again, a new light had entered her eyes. She told us about a place in Chelsea where she thought the two of us would have a good time. It was a club just for girls, though it was owned by a man who'd won the place from two businessmen in a poker game at the Dorchester. Syd had been going there on Saturday nights for a long time, back when the place was a mixed bunch – Jews, Blacks, gays, working ladies and lesbians. The word lesbian rang in my ears. I had never heard anyone say the word out loud. She began to rattle off names of patrons as if we'd know who she was talking about, bohemians who'd painted murals on the walls. Now it was mostly women, Syd told us, who liked it for the privacy and the pub prices. All we would have to do is dress well and be good-natured and we could be ourselves there. Our real selves, she said.

As we hurried home, Clara started planning our route across town, what lies to tell, what to wear. I tuned out of her chatter, my mind returning to the word *lesbian*. I'd read about homosexual scandals in Samuel's newspapers, but no one ever wrote about us girls. It was like we didn't exist. The knowledge that there was a place just for us thrilled me. I was convinced there was another life waiting for me. I just had to find it.

I squeezed Clara's hand distractedly when we said goodbye. My mind was already on a future that did not include her.

After I drive Kiki to the station, I decide to make chicken soup for Joanna.

It is my mother's recipe. *Goldene yoykh*, golden broth. This soup glistens and comforts and heals like no other. It is the stalwart of any good *baleboste* and if I am to exorcise my mother's voice then surely this is the way, confronting her head on.

But I can't help myself and play with the recipe, deviate from tradition. I peel a handful of garlic cloves and smash them into a paste with lemon juice, lemon pulp and a nub of salted butter. I rub this all over the chicken's pink and wrinkled skin. I stuff an onion into its backside. The chicken is enormous. I place it in a large casserole dish with carrots, celery, parsnip and dill and cover it all with an inch of cold water.

The soup rolls along on a gentle simmer. I clean the mess Kiki left in the bathroom and then return to the pot to skim off the foam.

When the flesh is falling away from the bone, I remove

everything from the pot and leave it to cool. The kitchen smells of dill and garlic.

I feed the dogs.

When the soup is cool, I strain it through a fine-mesh sieve, pick the chicken carcass clean with my fingers and coarsely chop the meat and vegetables into bite-size chunks and return them to the broth.

I am not sure that Joanna is going to like this recipe. She is a minimal eater at the best of times. But this is one of the only ways I can provide.

'I made chicken soup for dinner,' I announce as she sweeps into the kitchen in a smoky cloud of Shalimar, wool slacks and black cashmere turtleneck, gold glinting all over her body.

She takes a seat on the banquette, kisses me. 'Smells yummy.'

I've buttered some bread rolls and Joanna gently scrapes hers off. She is delicate as she takes her first taste of the soup and then wrinkles her nose. 'Is this something *Jewish*, darling?'

I shrug. She does not understand, or perhaps does not care to know the links to my past life. I open a bottle of Morgan and pour generous measures. We eat in silence, reading the Sunday papers, and then retire to the living room with another bottle for dessert. I light the fire as Joanna flicks through the TV guide.

The door bursts open and the dogs bound in. Mitzi, Coco and Betsey circle each other, our feet, then the coffee table, yapping and jumping until they discover where best they'd like to sit. Mitzi chooses to sidle up to my thigh. Coco prefers Joanna's lap. Betsey collapses on the rug in front of the log fire. Belly up, she stretches languidly, inviting warmth.

I realise I am stiff from trampolining when I feel the second bottle of wine relax my muscles. Or perhaps sitting for Kiki has set my limbs in a particular shape and they've been holding on to the arrangement. I don't have Kiki's fancy education but I'm no fool: when she talks of female artists harnessing their stories and their bodies, she is challenging my process of biting my tongue, of deflecting my history. It is quietly confrontational. She has got under my skin.

Joanna and I tune into a Sunday evening BBC police drama. I have no idea what's going on – some poor woman has been brutally murdered, there's a dodgy cop – but I'm still sober enough to notice we've nearly finished the wine. The glare of the TV is messing with my head. Joanna strokes my hand distractedly and asks who I think is the rat.

I shrug, pluck a random name.

When the phone rings, Joanna sighs and mutes the TV to answer it. She covers the receiver with her hand. 'Your sister,' she mouths, lips berry-stained, dry.

I swallow hard. Cold, cold dread in my guts.

I take the receiver, stare at it before placing it against my ear. I pick at a thread which is coming loose on one of the scatter cushions.

'Simone?'

There's silence for a moment and then she says, 'She finally did it, Edie. She's gone.'

I wait for something to break inside of me.

I stay intact.

'When?'

'This afternoon. I went to check on her after she still hadn't picked up the phone.'

'You found her?'

'In bed, yes.'

I swallow again. I see a floral pillow. A grey perm. Grey skin. Or is it blue? Silence as I try to find a way to reply.

'After all these years of talking about it,' Simone says, shock still in her voice, 'she goes and ODs on Valium on her birthday. Three bottles. Three.' Simone forces out something like a laugh. 'She meant business.'

I've often imagined my mother's death. Each time, I gave her alternative endings. Various dramatic methods by which to die, like a choose-your-own-adventure story. I never chose pills.

'She's gone?'

'She's gone.'

A kind of marvel to me: the woman I remember lived her life taking up as much space as she could, stretching out, ballooning into corners, going wherever she wanted at whatever time she desired, holding herself unaccountable to obligation, currying no favours, never shackling herself to the convention of politeness. She did not care what I, or my sister, thought of her, nor society in general. She waved goodbye to her judgemental friends. She divorced at a time when divorce was scandal absolute. Eventually, she ate like a glutton. More more more more more more.

What I mean is, she knew how to *live*. But she never seemed to enjoy it.

I don't speak, don't press my sister for any more details. I've heard enough.

'Are you there?' Simone asks.

'I'm here.'

'You should book a train. You need to come to the funeral.'

'She would hate that.'

'Exactly.'

We fall silent again. I don't know how to speak with my sister when it's not idle gossip. I send my love down the phone. I tell her that she sounds exhausted. That she should get some rest. We'll speak again in the morning. There are so many things I do not say.

I hang up.

I wonder what I've lost.

I thought I'd lost everything already.

And then I wonder if she has left me any money.

'Oh darling,' Joanna says when I tell her the news. She moves closer to me on the sofa. 'I'm sorry.' She strokes my hand. A few minutes pass, her soft skin against my rough skin.

She replenishes her glass, then mine. And then she says, 'Let's do hope she isn't the haunting kind,' and turns the TV volume back up.

I stare at her. 'My mother has been haunting me all my life.'

'What can I say, darling? She was a terrible mother. The absolute worst. Good riddance to bad rubbish.' She squeezes my hand again. 'Speaking of which, would you be a dear?'

She passes me the empty wine bottle.

Lyra found me outside the wrong entrance to the Gateways club. I'd tried and tried to locate the green door, scouring the King's Road, cold to the bone. She asked how old I was and how I'd found out about the place and when I was too stunned to answer she flashed a lopsided grin, took my hand, and led me through a gate and down a steep set of stairs. I couldn't have imagined so many women together. Dancing, touching, kissing! I was so excited I didn't stop to feel bad about Clara. Clara, who I'd lied to for the first time, who I knew I was about to deeply betray.

I soon spent every Saturday night there. Chelsea wasn't far by Tube but it was like falling down the rabbit hole every time I stepped out at Sloane Square. Buildings sharply outlined against the sky, bustle below as long-haired, flamboyantly dressed men and women criss-crossed the crowded streets. They were painters, novelists, *bon vivants*. I was sixteen. Full of hungry energy.

Gateways was humid and rollicking by 9 p.m., brightly coloured walls barely visible through the smoke. Bodies packed in tight, sweating and swaying. I had such tenderness for all of them, friends and strangers, the gentle palm on my back as someone squeezed past me on their way to the bar. Women were banned from wearing trousers in most restaurants but at the club you could wear what you wanted as long as you made an effort. I loved how I felt in trousers. No suspender belts, nothing sucking me in. I'd turned my father's old slacks into drainpipes and paired them with shirts with separate collars attached with studs.

Lyra was not beautiful. Angular and lanky, all arms and legs and heavy lashes eclipsing small eyes. But things happened around her. Electric things. Incredible things. She was a revelation, ten years my senior, hair so fair it looked silver. She'd broken off an engagement to a rich broker and lived on her own terms. When she wasn't at the Gates, she drank at the Pier Hotel with her gay friends. She lived in a tiny bedsit in Earl's Court. Her world was a thousand times bigger than mine.

The Sensations were on the jukebox because they were always on the jukebox that summer. I danced with Lyra, my leg between hers as we moved in sync. I could feel the warmth of her pussy on my thigh. Next to us were Doreen and Ray. They were lost in each other, eyes closed, mouths on necks. Doreen was a prostitute. Her butch was Ray and she used him as her protective. Ray bound his breasts with a girdle and stuffed socks into his briefs. He was magnificent.

'Will you get me a drink, honey?' Lyra murmured into my ear.

Lyra never went up to the bar by herself. She worked full time at a florist's so she could afford to buy a round, but she was my girl and this meant I got the drinks, whether she slipped me the cash or I paid with the little money I earned at the pharmacy. I wanted to seduce; Lyra wanted to be seduced. It was perfect. In bed though, the roles were reversed. She spent hours on me. Clara had never put her mouth on my clit, but Lyra showed me how to use tongues. Tongues and hands. She wore a charm bracelet on her right wrist with four gold elephants dangling from the chain and when she fingered me it jangled like Santa's sleigh. *Christmas, Christmas, Christmas* it whispered as I came.

I'd separated myself from school and Clara in one fell swoop, giving up on my studies and switching my crush. My boss at the pharmacy liked me. He thought I had *chutzpah* and promised to train me up. I was grateful for the money but couldn't imagine staying there dealing with people's piles or hacking coughs which sent spittle flying across the counter. Any free moments were spent poring over catalogues looking at ties and tailored suits and silk scarves for Lyra.

I joined the queue at the bar and ordered myself a lager shandy and a sweet sherry. The bartender was broad-shouldered, small and fair with freckled skin. She lived with the owner and his wife and child, a set-up which was the subject of constant debate among the rest of us. The small sink beside her was full of soapy water, the foam grey from piles of dirty ashtrays. As I waited my turn, a pretty woman approached one of the butches next to me, a heavy-muscled tank, and asked if she could borrow his wife for a dance. 'Best of luck to you,' he quipped. 'She wears me out.' No one ever asked me if they could dance with Lyra – they took without asking. I was still the squirt, figuring it all out. At least Lyra never did more than dance.

I handed over my cash and made my way across the room to where Lyra was sitting at a table with Phyllis and Marie.

'He's terrible,' Lyra was saying to Marie. 'I don't know how you manage him.'

Phyllis and Marie had been a couple for years but they were in lavender marriages with gay men. Lyra said it was to protect themselves from family pressure and suspicion from people at work, but I knew she pitied them, having to share their homes with the opposite sex and not each other. I didn't think it so repulsive to live with a man. Sometimes, when I woke to Simone's baby cries at night, memories of my father needled me in the dark. The herby smell of his shaving foam, his baritone echoing through the flat, how he lightly pinched my right earlobe. The way he had neutralised my mother. Most of all, I missed looking at his face and seeing my own features blinking back at me.

'What he lacks in general housekeeping, he makes up for in cooking,' Marie said.

'Edie is an excellent cook,' Lyra said, smiling, taking her sherry. I kissed Phyllis and Marie on the cheek and sat beside Lyra, slipping an arm around her shoulder. She saw me fumbling in my pockets for a lighter and immediately produced a heavy silver Zippo for my Pall Mall and nudged the ashtray in my direction. I sat back, inhaled deeply.

'I couldn't do it,' Lyra was saying. 'Not after what my father did to me. I couldn't share a roof with any kind of man.'

I exhaled. 'Did he beat you? You never said.'

Phyllis shot me a stern look.

'You don't know?' Marie asked me. She looked at Lyra, who shook her head.

'Know what?'

'He put her in a head hospital,' Marie said quietly. 'Against her will and all. Said he'd make her a ward of court if not.'

Lyra sipped her sherry. 'You're lucky your father left before he realised you're a les girl,' she said. 'When mine found me fooling around, he sent me off to be treated for sexual deviancy. You know what they did to me in there?' She drained the rest of her sherry. 'They strapped me in a chair and showed me pictures. Every few were of naked women. When a woman flashed up, they injected something into my arm which made me vomit. I threw up each time I saw a naked woman. They thought it would cure me. I was sick for months.'

I swallowed hard, reached for Lyra's hand. Suddenly all the freedom I felt at the club was terrifying. The world shrank back down to those like me, and those against me. The scales so unbalanced.

'Thing is,' Lyra continued, 'none of those pictures were even sexy to me. I don't go in for femmes. The whole thing was rigged to what men think a sexy woman looks like.'

'They get us all wrong, of course,' Phyllis said.

Lyra turned to me. I was trembling. 'It's okay, Edie,' she said into my ear. 'It's over now. Me and my pa don't speak anymore. And look, their damn treatment didn't do a thing. I'm as big a les as ever.' She kissed the side of my face. 'Let's dance again. Please? Forget this horribleness.'

We moved out onto the floor and I took her in my arms, guiding us around confidently. Someone put a slow song on the jukebox, and Lyra rested her head on my shoulder. Despite our age difference, I was determined to not let anything like that happen to her again. I said as much, whispering soft words to her, the softest ones I knew. Lyra nuzzled the side of my neck. But I couldn't shake my unease. I was at home at Gateways but the wider world was not ready for me. I saw how many of the women here were leading a double life – and I was one of them. My mother was harbouring a subversive. She just didn't know it.

As we emerged into the warm night, I was telling Lyra about my craving for crêpes Suzette when I saw Samuel leaning against the street lamp, watching the wrong door, waiting. Even before he saw me his face was twisted with shame. There was only one person in the world who'd know where I was and tell my mother. Only one person who wanted to hurt me that much.

Clara, Lyra. Such a simple, fatal, slip of the tongue. I didn't know how much Clara cared until I called her by the wrong name. I didn't know she really loved me.

As Samuel walked towards us, I floated up and away from my body until I felt Lyra grip my arm harder and whisper, 'Who is that man?'

Samuel stood in front us now, head bowed, unable to look me in the eye. He was shaking. I was shaking. I was saying *no, no, no, no* but not a single word came out.

'I'm sorry, Edie,' he said, pulling me away from Lyra who was shouting at him to fuck off. 'Your mother has already packed your bags.'

I pieced it all together in slow motion as he bundled me into the back of his banged-up Citroën. Clara's face white with fury, her walk to the payphone at the end of my road, how breathless she must have been dialling our number while I, too, was breathless, dancing on the slippery floor so happy and oh God, Clara, please don't do it, I am begging you, please Clara, I'm sorry I left you behind, but Samuel picks up the phone on the third ring, worried by the late hour, and Clara takes a deep breath and spits, *Your daughter isn't sleeping at mine. Your daughter is a dirty lesbian*, and with that she says the name of the club and slams down the receiver, and I'm still on the dance floor laughing, and Clara sobs because she knows she won't ever be able to take this back, because she knows my mother was listening the whole time and she will send Samuel out to find me, to bring me home, so that she can tell me that this isn't my home anymore.

'You have no idea of the danger you are to yourself,' Samuel said, putting his key in the ignition.

My head filled with blood and I thought, where is your big heart now, Samuel? Where is all the love you learned to hold on to during the war?

And then I thought about Syd in Clara's building. How we'd never seen anyone visit her. Not a single person, male or female, entering or leaving her flat in all that time we watched and waited for her to acknowledge us.

No one.

She was entirely on her own.

I walk to the edge of the beach where the smallest pebbles meet the grey water. Somewhere behind me, the dogs are chasing each other. Their yips and barks of joy break across the wind and arrive at my ears fractured and jumbled.

I spent the night holding the fact of my mother's death in my mind. At dawn I gave up on sleep and drove to the water on autopilot, bundled in an old Barbour jacket and wellies. There's no one here this early in the morning. Not even the mad swim club who begin each day immersed in the freezing cold. The waves roll and break against the shore and I can feel them roll through my body, licking my most tender spots. For all the years I've lived by the coast I have seen my mother's anger in these waves, a motion which builds on itself, deepening, affirming. Now that she is dead, a part of me is surprised to see the waves are still rocking with fury.

Silence between two people is easy to grow. It's not that it doesn't need tending. It takes a certain effort to ignore the impulse to speak, to incite, to defend. But now it is infinite. I don't need to try anymore.

Mitzi crashes across the beach and drops her ball at my feet. She pants, expectant. I pick it up, throw as hard as I can and she follows its trajectory as it arches across the dull sky, her mouth snapping, ready to retrieve.

I have wanted to be free of my mother's judgement all my life. Now she's gone, I've got what I wanted. And yet. No new, liberated form. If anything, the cracks in me have widened and I'm afraid of what's waiting to rush in.

TWO

What followed my expulsion from Carlton Mansions surprised me. Rather than becoming a free spirit, liberated from the tyranny of my mother's moods, I instead set about forcing fierce attachments, stifling Lyra as Clara had once stifled me, spending every night at Gateways, asking for more hours at the pharmacy. It didn't take long for Lyra to leave me. Without her, I was broke, struggling with the rent on a tiny bedsit. To make ends meet I stole from work. It didn't take long to get caught.

I only ever phoned my mother once. I made the call from Kensington police station. I'd been arrested for writing cheques that I knew would bounce. Ironically, I needed money to make bail, pay the fine and avoid prison.

I trembled when I heard my mother announce her full name and my old telephone number. One, two, three seconds passed before I mustered the courage to speak. When my mother heard my voice she hung up.

I turned to the police officer, shaken.

'Put down the phone, did she?' she asked. 'Bet you've run that mother of yours ragged. Go on, have one more go.'

I swallowed. There was no one else I could call.

I dialled again.

This time Samuel answered. I didn't recognise myself as I mumbled my way through an explanation. The police officer was smirking.

'I'll be there in an hour,' Samuel said curtly. There was a pause. 'Your mother has asked you not to call again.'

I didn't hang up straight away but listened to the dial tone. I thought of Clara and the red phone box on the corner of Randolph Avenue.

Samuel arrived with a cheque that didn't bounce. Fifteen minutes later, I was released. Out on the street, I caught sight of him sitting in his red Citroën. He looked so much older. Living with my mother could do that to a person.

To keep my bedsit, I got a job with Ray, the pimp at Gateways, putting postcards in phone boxes for his prostitutes. For three years, it felt like my fate pivoted on phone boxes. I lived on Turkish flatbreads and tinned meat.

I have always admired a woman with a healthy appetite. It's why I still love London even though she ate me alive. Since I've been away, the city has fed its irrevocable hunger for concrete. It grows, unrelenting. The clashing skyline of trees and blocks of flats and motionless cranes rushes past the smeary window until my train pulls into St Pancras, drawing its length along the platform before staggering to a halt.

On the plastic pull-down table are two empty red wine miniatures and a stained paperback of *Giovanni's Room* – a book I've read, and re-read, for thirty years. Each time my heart breaks for Giovanni in a new way. It breaks for Giovanni but what of my mother? Simone has planned the funeral and the shiva. All I have to do is show up. Show up without showing myself up.

It took me a day to decide to come. Joanna was bemused by my indecision. If it was her, she said, she wouldn't go. There was no question of Joanna accompanying me, not with *my* family history – besides, *the dogs*. She did pack my luggage. An act of kindness, though it leaves me at the mercy of her taste. But a day spent deliberating is like a week for Jewish deaths. The soul neither on earth nor ready to be admitted to heaven until it hits the dust. No reason to let our loved ones' souls hover around their dead body, distressed and disorientated. Get them to the ground sharpish so they can return to heaven. I know all this and yet there is a gap where faith should be. I'll admit – I have sensed a presence over me, something watching and judging, but I always assumed it was my mother.

Tonight, I'll stay with Simone. I had an option with the trains: St Pancras or Victoria. The Victoria route is faster, but its tracks would have taken me through Earl's Court and I was fearful of what fresh memories would have announced themselves. I haven't set eyes on Earl's Court in decades, not since the year I spent there with Lyra, cobbling some kind of life together from poorly paid jobs, all communing flesh, swinging hair, brandy, dancing, summer passing into rattling windowpanes and hissing, leaking radiators, so squeezed into that tiny flat it squeezed out all our affection. Less like being in the heart of the city than in its churning, unpredictable bowels. Funny, really, how sensitive I feel about certain parts of London, as if the life I led then will return if I step on the same ground.

I gather my belongings and step out onto the platform. Arrival and departure boards flicker, suitcases and backpacks bump my sides; perfumes and body odour mingle with food smells. In the days when we still travelled, Joanna and I had a driver take us from Broadstairs to London, his eyes on the road, discreet. We'd lounge in the leather seats, smoking, sipping a half-bottle of Moët. Not Joanna's favourite kind of champagne but pleasant enough for the journey, she'd said. I loved our time alone in the back of whichever Mercedes or BMW was driving that day. Travelling towards the city meant travelling towards Harry and his friends' parties but those two, three hours of speeding along tarmac alone with Joanna were bliss. I have still never seen her on a train.

I find my feet. I follow the signs northbound to Finsbury Park. It's been so long since I've stepped onto an escalator.

The Underground is hot and airless and there is a special kind of fever that emanates from Christmas shoppers. So many different kinds of faces. I wonder what age will have done to Simone's face. I've never seen where she lives with her family. I've never even met her daughter. The funeral is tomorrow morning and then my mother will also be underground. It's not possible for her to be cremated, of course, not with the chambers. But I'm sure her spirit will find a way to be disgruntled with her plot, reprimand neighbouring bodies for decomposing too slowly, their hair still growing, encroaching on her space.

Outside, the air is bitter. A young woman is cross-legged on the pavement, the bus station rising up behind her with its plastic shelters. She can't be more than eighteen years old, with no shelter, just a blanket, a book and a cardboard sign asking for money or food. I drop a few coins into her coffee cup. She murmurs thanks. I'm about to turn away when I bend down and press my copy of

Giovanni's Room into her hands. 'It's very good,' I say. She smiles.

I pull out the Post-it note with Simone's directions. Blackstock Road is swarming with people. Bric-a-brac shops, a greengrocer, halal butcher, café after café with rows of baklava and creamy patisserie in the window. I turn right onto a tree-lined side street and then right again. There is her house. Or, more accurately, there is her top-floor flat. It looks the same as the other Georgian houses along this terrace, except across one side ivy is trying to cover the cracks in the walls.

I have the feeling I might stand in front of this door forever when a young voice calls out, 'Hello.'

I glance around; the street is empty. A giggle. I look up. A girl's face is at an open window. She looks so much like my little sister that I stumble backwards onto the kerb. 'Careful,' she warns.

When I was little, my mother invested a lot of hope in my future. She wanted a better life for me than she'd had in Odessa – a desire that did not play out with warmth or encouragement, but a desire nonetheless. She never saw what became of that hope. Never knew if I suffered or grew sick. If my heart had been broken, of if I had found love, a calling. If I had thrived. I look at this girl's open face which borrows the bones of my sister's face which borrows the bones of our mother's face and consider all the simple things my mother might have known about her grown-up daughter. Where my new moles are, how early my periods stopped, the names of my dogs. Whether it had been a life of ease or difficulty. How on earth I ended up with Joanna.

The girl is staring. She seems puzzled.

'Hi Anais,' I say, 'I'm Edie. Aunt Edie, I guess.' The word *aunt* feels strange in my mouth. For so long Joanna has been my only family.

She giggles again. 'I know, silly. Are you coming in?'

I met Joanna at a New Year's Eve party in West Kensington. I was with my friend Annie, who was a friend of the host. By 10 p.m. I was already so drunk I had to keep one eye shut to stop seeing double. The party was full of people like Annie: good jobs, good genes, good connections. I say Annie was my friend, but really she was a client – I met her at the pharmacy where I filled her Valium prescription. When she became too dozy to look after the kids, I sold her purple hearts on the side. She paid a good chunk of my rent that way.

Annie thought it hip to know a young dyke pill-pusher. She invited me to London society parties where she'd flirt with me in front of her husband's friends. She wore her red hair in a beehive thick with lacquer which would stay the course while the rest of her got loose. She was beautiful, but not my type. I'd eat and drink all I desired and pick up a few new customers, so I didn't mind being her *exotic* sidekick. But by the time I met Joanna it was dawning on me that there was only so long you could survive on the outside.

Out on the balcony, I lit a Pall Mall and watched the smoke disappear among the rows of identical houses where silhouettes cavorted across misted windows. My arms turned to chicken skin. The door opened – a burst of laughter and jazz trumpets – before clicking shut again.

'May I borrow a light?' A voice thick like tar, lustrous and sensual.

I turned. She was backlit, a glowing pageboy haircut, champagne-coloured catsuit, nipples hard knots beneath the fabric. But it was her eyes that got me: bright, raw, the deepest blue I'd ever seen. It was hard to tell her age – she was too well groomed. Thirty, maybe? Older than me. I checked her wedding finger. An enormous oval sapphire the same colour as her eyes. She played with a silver pendant at her chest, fingering it tenderly while she waited for me to reply.

I took my Zippo, offered the flame to the tip of her Marlboro Red. She inhaled deeply, rubbed her arms. She watched the misted party scene playing out across the window of the opposite house. 'They look like ghosts through all that condensation,' she said, blowing out cigarette smoke in an elegant stream.

'I can relate.'

'To ghosts?'

I shrugged. 'Don't you ever feel transparent? Invisible? Maybe I'm just bored of crashing parties.'

'I've seen you before. Aren't you a friend of Annie's?'

'I'm her pharmacist.'

She smiled, extended her free hand and introduced

herself. I wanted to run my tongue along those ballerina-pink nails.

There was a sudden crash as two people slammed against the door in a dancing frenzy. I slipped another cigarette from the pack. Joanna narrowed her eyes, stepped closer. 'I hope you don't mind me saying, darling, but you don't look very well,' she said. 'A touch grey.'

I pulled a face. 'Ghostly?'

Joanna laughed, then looked thoughtful. 'Hosts *need* guests in order to provide their hospitality. Where would Kenneth and his fabulous apartment be without you? Empty, save for that awful rat he calls a dog. He needs an audience.' She took another drag of her cigarette. 'Host, guest, stranger all share the same root word *ghos-ti*. So you're entitled to be both guest *and* stranger if you like – either way, you're entangled with Kenneth, the host. It takes three.'

I blew out smoke, grinned.

'Now come on,' she said, 'let's not be maudlin. Time for dessert.' She took my hand like we were old friends and wrenched open the door.

The heat hit like a wave. The room was dimly lit, air thick with incense and smoke. Bookshelves lined an entire wall; the others were painted orange and decorated with Afghan tapestries and block-colour canvases which I'd later learn were Rothkos. Joanna weaved us through the dance floor, crowded with glistening bodies. A Saudi prince commandeered the centre of the room, surrounded by svelte women with legs like gazelles. They were shrieking and holding on to each other, dipping their jutting shoulders and snaking their hips to 'Honky Tonk Women'.

She led me to the table where food lay in high piles. Duck terrine, quiches, shrimp, lamb cutlets, dozens of cheeses. At the dessert table we both went for the poached pears. The fruit halves swam in a red-wine liquor studded with cardamon pods and star anise, generous mounds of mascarpone floating on top. I took a spoon to the tender flesh and scooped.

'That's Harry,' she said, pointing at a heavyset man in a smoking tuxedo I immediately coveted. He was opening a bottle of Bollinger, a young woman in a sequinned dress clinging to his shoulder. 'My husband,' Joanna explained.

I raised an eyebrow. The cork popped and the bottle fizzed over.

'Don't be fooled by the young thing hanging from him – she's studying mathematics at Oxford. Very bright, too bright for Harry.'

'You don't mind?'

'A little distraction goes a long way, darling. One must always appreciate life's little gifts.'

Harry must have felt our eyes on him because he turned and came over with the bottle. He was perhaps a decade older than Joanna, handsome and solid like an aging rugby-player, but with red pockmarked jowls and the kind of sheen that comes from years of excess and being very, very sure of yourself.

'Who's your new pal?' he asked.

Joanna introduced us and Harry grasped my hand firmly

and squeezed. When he pulled away, a layer of grease was left on my palm. He poured three glasses and beckoned us to a velvet couch where he immediately began to tell me about his textile empire. I knocked back my drink.

When Joanna explained I worked in a pharmacy, his eyes lit up. 'You must meet a lot of characters.'

'I meet a lot of liars.'

Harry burst out laughing. 'I like this one. She's a hoot.'

'What I'd like to know,' Joanna said, speaking to both of us, or neither of us, I wasn't sure, 'is how to define the difference between a secret and a lie. I feel that secrets are more benevolent, but I'm sure many people would argue all secrets involve lies.' She took a sip of champagne. 'Secrets can be useful, though. They're perfect stand-ins for boundaries. They draw invisible lines in the sand that can't be crossed.'

'My old lady is very secretive,' Harry said. 'She even keeps secrets in her jewellery.'

Joanna lifted the pendant from her chest, turning it on its side before popping open the clasp and removing a tiny silver spoon. She scooped out a small mound of white powder and offered it to Harry. He dipped his head and pressed a finger against one nostril, snorting hard. She repeated the action and then smiled at me, her eyes even more electric, more dazzling. I leaned over, my face next to her breast, surprised by the pungent scent of Shalimar, and sniffed.

A few seconds and then a warm stirring in my fingertips. The beat of the music went through me. I began to pulse like the rest of the room. Harry slipped his arm around Joanna's tiny waist and squeezed. I was intent on getting close to her. Desire so strong my mind might as well have been blank.

We talked and talked and either I can't remember, or I was never really listening, but I've no memory of what we spoke about, only that we stayed on that couch for hours, snorting and talking, my brain busy plotting how to get in between them, imagining how Joanna's mouth would taste like butterscotch.

At some point, Harry took Joanna's hand, the one with the sapphire ring, and placed it on my knee. I smiled, all slow, unhurried although my heart was pounding in that chemical way. Womph womph womph.

If only I could have floated up high enough to see what the three of us looked like, what a scene we struck as our lives came together, how we were already leaving behind a barely perceptible trace of chaos, like the slime trail of three criss-crossing slugs.

Host, guest, stranger.

Ghost.

Slicing a piece of Simone's meatloaf, the thought arrives like a brief seizure: dead to me and dead – these *are* two different things.

For the first time, my mother is not actually in this world. Before, there was always the possibility we'd see each other again. A coincidence. Both staring into the same dessert fridge of a Marks & Spencer Foodhall deliberating over chocolate eclairs or a treacle tart. Lane to lane on the M25, glancing sideways as our cars glide away, one overtaking the other. Was it . . . ? Could it be . . . ? But, no – my mother never learned to drive. Perhaps we'd be called for the same jury service, placed at the heart of a murder trial, instructed to decide the fate of some poor soul when our own souls were so blackened and lacking. Or maybe it would be deliberate. A knock at Damson Manor one rainy night. *Surprise!* In those fantasies, which I thought I'd long since stopped entertaining, I can hear her whisper *mamele, mamele,* as she strokes my curls. She falls to her knees and in a mix of Yiddish and English proclaims, *Edie,* ziskayt, *I am so—*

But here the image falters, stops short.

I cannot even imagine my mother saying sorry. I have turned her into another woman completely. How like Zelda to rip up my dream world.

So, as I prod the grey meat, half listening to Arnold, Simone's husband, talk about golf, I realise what I've lost is the sweetness of possible reconciliation. Serendipity is the real closed door. All those hours spent ruminating turned to dust. It is a shock to feel this pain. I avoid Simone's eyes. It's too hard to look directly at them. They are dark and expressive like our mother's.

When Anais asks if I'm okay I realise she's been watching me. I nod, take another sip of red wine. Tall for her age and dressed in stonewash jeans and a black turtleneck, Anais is already showing glimpses of what her teenage self will look like. Those round cheeks will melt away to reveal more of the high cheekbones of her mother. The chin will harden.

Arnold and my sister are doing a fantastic job of acting normally. I have to concede how comfortable it feels to be sitting at their round dinner table. The ease with which we pass the salt, replenish each other's water glasses. I have spent so many hours on the phone with Simone, have become so familiar with the details of their life, it's as if we've shared the same house. I know which cabinet stores the wedding china, how many times the boiler has broken. I even know what this place cost. And yet, how hard it is for me to join these details together to make a whole life. How different the cabinet looks from the one I'd imagined. Uglier. The whole flat more modern than I expected. There are only four framed photographs. Three of Anais at different ages, all of which I have copies of, and one of Simone and Arnold's wedding day. None of our mother. Her aged face is still a mystery to me.

Anais goes back to her book. She has been reading *The Secret Garden* throughout dinner, head bent, brown hair falling over her thick eyelashes. She isn't bothered about a strange family member appearing at her home for the first time.

Simone clears the plates and brings out a fruit salad in a cut-crystal bowl. Grapes, kiwi, orange and apple segments slosh around in mixed juices, and I'm touched by this offer. I know how long it takes to slice each fruit carefully. We chew. We chatter. I pour myself more wine. I am so damn grateful for the wine.

But when Anais goes up for a bath and Arnold leaves to tend to the dishes, my sister switches gears and launches into the funeral plans. She has found a rabbi willing to bury our mother despite her mode of death. I blink in response. I hadn't given thought to religious law, how suicide disobeys the highest Jewish duty of preserving life. Those of our mother's generation would call for the body to be buried outside of the cemetery. I can imagine what the women of Carlton Mansions would have to say. *The Kaddish is pushing it, just a few simple words of mourning and that's it. Goodnight, Zelda. Shame on those who dare to rob God of his property. And a woman who lived through the Holocaust years, no less.* Except they never used that word: Holocaust.

And yet I remember enough of my schooling to recall famous examples of suicide in Jewish history. Take King Saul, who killed himself rather than face torture or forced conversion at the hands of the Philistines. Or the Jews who occupied the fortress of Masada and committed mass suicide to avoid surrendering to the Romans. These suicides have been venerated as acts of bravery and self-sacrifice. But what of the old woman who simply tired of life? There are some ways to get around this blasphemy if needed. Compulsion – a rash decision born of a multiplicity of troubles, pain or poverty – is forgiven. Only someone who killed themselves knowingly, in Hebrew *lada'at*, someone of sound mind, is considered by Jewish law to have truly committed suicide. This person must be clear-headed and announce their intention to take their own life.

How much does this help my mother?

One thing that is certain: my mother was erratic, not clear-headed. But according to my sister she did announce her desire to die for forty-odd years. Surely that is undisputable intention. Murky waters indeed.

Simone asks if I'm paying attention. She has made many lists. I'm sure they are comforting to her but they scare the shit out of me. How does she have so many practical thoughts and enough energy to organise them? She reads from a leather notebook, sucking on the tip of a biro. It is fast becoming clear that my mother was short of friends. They are all dead, or aggrieved, or else dead *and* aggrieved, and Simone is worried the prayer hall will be empty. I let the details sink in. She will be buried alongside Samuel,

Simone's father, in their joint plot at Edgwarebury Cemetery where the West London Synagogue own land. I agree with the flower choices. I agree with the music choices. I agree with the fish balls and mini salmon bagels; the egg rolls, and cream cheese and cucumber rolls, the array of pastries for shiva. I make a mental note of when I need to wake up tomorrow, what time we'll leave.

We will need to decide on the gravestone, Simone tells me, whether we want to dedicate a rose tree in her name, or a hardwood bench with a brass plaque. It is all business, this dying business. It is expensive and demanding and shaming. What tokens to bestow. How much to spend. Our mother is dead and life goes on. Life that is inane and unfair and full of decisions that must be made.

There is no talk of the will. I cannot bring myself to ask for fear of the answer. Financial freedom. There is too much to hope for.

'Simone,' I say when she pauses for air. 'Do you feel Jewish?'

She lets out a breath. '*That's* your question?'

'All this fuss over tradition. Is it because you believe or because it was how you were raised?'

She narrows her eyes. 'You don't have to believe. You're just as Jewish if you believe or don't believe. God doesn't care. As long as you follow his word.'

'You don't think God cares if there's nothing in my heart?'

'I reckon there's plenty in your heart for you to be getting on with.'

Simone tops up her wine, then mine, puts the bottle back on the table but does not take her hand from the neck. She swallows, and then tells me that there was no note. She delivers this piece of news as if it was worse than the suicide itself. I couldn't care less that there was no note. In fact, I am relieved. I don't want to hear my mother yell at me from beyond the grave.

'Her heart was so strong,' Simone blurts out. 'The heart of an ox.' She sets her hands on the table. They are shaking.

The heart of an ox. Does she know oxen are castrated male cattle? I recall how on the phone Simone often described our mother as doing *unreasonably well*. I touch her hand, feel the muscles relax.

Simone grips my palm and tells me Arnold will go back to work after the shiva. 'Will you stay the week?' she says. 'Help me clear the flat? She has . . . a lot of stuff. She became something of a shopaholic.'

I hesitate, trying to imagine a week in this life. Before I can answer, Simone begins talking again. I can see she is surprised by her own outburst and retreats back into planning mode: what would I like for breakfast, do I need an iron for my outfit? As soon as she takes a breath, I ask if I can sleep on it – the idea of staying beyond the funeral – and whether she'd mind if I got an early night. I am not lying when I say it has been a long day. All I want is a cool pillow and a heavy duvet. A little respite from my thoughts.

'Absolutely,' she says. Simone understands, of course she understands. This is the woman who earlier greeted me like we'd had coffee last week. Who pulled me in close, kissed both my cheeks and welcomed me into her pristine home. Who showed me to the guest room so I could drop my bag, patting a small double bed with four plump pillows, cotton sheets so smooth they must have been pressed. Poor Joanna got the wrong sister – Simone's flat is impeccable. It was not so much a reunion as a non-event. If I'd been afraid of any awkwardness between us, it was a fear misplaced. Nothing of consequence about Simone has changed. A few more lines, more demure clothing. Still practical, still kind, her motherly qualities now directed to the right recipient in Anais. She is still my little sister. Any criticism she may have made about my life fades to nothing as I recall kissing her pudgy baby feet as they kicked, joyfully, in the air.

I cannot sleep, of course. I haven't spent a night away from Damson Manor in a decade and there is no Joanna lying next to me, reading or dozing, or looking so good I slide down the sheets and nestle between her legs. I try to focus on thoughts of her warm skin, but it's hard to even imagine being sexual in such a wholesome room, with its striped blinds and polished floor.

I wonder if Joanna misses me. She is not sentimental. Neither of us have a mobile phone so I called from Simone's landline when I arrived. A strange reversal, cradling my sister's handset. Joanna picked up the phone after several rings, announcing her name formally, followed by our number minus the area code. She sounded pleased to hear from me, asked if it was as weird as I'd thought. I said it wasn't. She told me about her exhausting walk with the dogs, asked me where the big wooden spoon was, chastising me for always putting things back in the wrong place. 'But I'm the big spoon,' I said. Silence. She did not find me funny. I told her the spoon was in the cupboard next to the dishwasher, wished her a lovely evening. She told me to hold my head high tomorrow.

Two decades of pseudo-marriage. That was all we had to say.

I train my eyes on the peak of the attic ceiling, regretting giving away my copy of *Giovanni's Room*, listening instead to the unfamiliar sounds of my family-not-family close up their flat for the night. The hum of the TV and then quiet. The toilet chain clangs against the wall when it's flushed, the pipes groan with the rush of water. A floorboard creaks. Simone and Arnold talk in hushed voices, a door opens and then closes as they check on Anais. Lights click off. Finally, they turn in themselves, and then there is true silence – something I never expected from an old Georgian building in the city.

And although everything is still and calm, all under control, all organised, my body feels like someone has pressed an emergency button. Nerve ends fired. Every bone lively. If this is grief, it's like a caffeine buzz. I'm hungry again. Where is all my sorrow?

I roll onto my side.

I wait to start feeling bad again.

I'd run out of cash the week Joanna called me for the first time. She'd got my number from Annie, who was only too happy to indulge a potential tryst. By then it was early spring. Harry and Joanna had been abroad on business for three months, their daughters at boarding school. I immediately loved the sound of Joanna's voice on the phone, honeyed and velvet.

For a restaurant so famous, it was smaller than I'd expected. I wore a black Christian Dior jacket with wide crêpe trousers – a gift from Annie after she'd lost more weight. My stomach pulsed as I followed the hostess weaving between the fifteen or so circular tables. Short white tablecloths floated like ghosts in the dim light.

Harry stood, pulled me to his chest, then stepped back to observe me as if I were a niece he hadn't seen since child-hood. 'Look at you,' he said, thumping the table with a fist. 'I don't even know what you are. It's marvellous. Sit down, Edie, sit. We've been looking forward to this all week.'

I sat across from them like a job interview. Him so solid, her so slight. Joanna was wearing an orange cape, mini skirt and go-go boots, a flash of pale thigh between skirt and leather. She smiled at me from under a shiny fringe which hung in a crescent around her eyes. A waiter sprang out of the dark and removed a bottle from a silver ice bucket.

Harry toasted to the three us. Crystal clinked. Bubbles burst in my throat. There was a plate of cured meat and olives in the centre and Harry reached for a slice and folded it into his mouth. I hadn't noticed before how his teeth were impossibly straight, impossibly white.

'So, Edie, friend of Annie,' he said, swallowing. 'Remind me, how did you meet our dear Anne Boleyn?'

'He calls her that because she's always losing her head,' Joanna said, and then smiled. 'Awfully mean.'

Poor Annie. I explained that she'd come into my pharmacy one Tuesday morning in search of hydrocortisone cream for her husband's eczema.

Harry snorted. 'Rock 'n' roll,' he said, slapping his thigh.

'It's around his throat,' I said, sitting up even straighter and imitating Annie's nasal voice, 'like a ghastly red scarf knitted by your grandmama.'

They laughed. I took a long drink of champagne. So much for defending my friend.

Joanna's hand fluttered over the water glass before resting in her lap. Her eyes darted around the room and then she opened her clutch, took out a pack of Marlboro and slid a cigarette from the box. Harry reached over and provided a flame. She puffed, exhaled a thick stream of smoke, and then asked me to tell them about the pharmacy.

'Joanna's fascinated by people's jobs,' Harry said. 'Not mine, of course. But everyone else's. It's only natural, I suppose, when one hasn't worked a day in one's life.'

She jabbed a slender finger in his belly and then leaned forward to rest her chin in her hands. I was surprised she put her elbows on the table.

I told them I had worked in pharmacies since I was fifteen, leaving out the time I'd been fired for stealing. I'd been at Adin's Pharmacy for the past two years. 'The owner is good to me,' I said. 'He says I remind him of his son in Turkey.'

Harry erupted into another guffaw. I could not stop staring at his shiny teeth.

I looked back at Joanna. She held my gaze. Her long lashes had been gathered into thick clumps, top and bottom, and she was slow to blink. The restaurant hummed around us.

I leaned in, the beginnings of pleasure stirring in my gut, the champagne doing its job. I told her Fridays were my favourite day. Not because it was the weekend – I worked Saturdays – but because every Friday morning I changed the window display. Mr Adin's late wife had an impressive collection of empty perfume bottles and it was my idea to use them in our window arrangements. The display set us apart from the competition and we attracted a particular kind of crowd. A glamorous old lady, Marine, came to see it every week. She wore a mink stole, no matter the weather, and brought me pistachio macarons. We chatted about perfume and her dead husband and all the places where her body hurt. She always left with beta blockers and cod liver oil.

Harry called over the waiter and ordered for the three of us. Joanna asked where I found the patience, talking to strangers all day, listening to their ailments.

I shrugged and explained how I'd grown up around a lot of women like Marine. And then I found myself going off script. I told her how my mother was a terrible hypochondriac. There was always some ailment from which she was suffering. Heart palpitations, gut ache, the somewhat abstract 'raw bones'. If she was either too hot, or too cold, it would be a fever and she'd take to bed. The problem would start benign, like a small cough, and become tuberculosis within the hour. When I was small, I'd have to accompany her to the doctor. She'd half drag me by the arm, sweating and moaning all the way. But as soon as she arrived at the consultation room it was like she could breathe again. She'd settle into the Formica chair and begin a meticulous litany of complaints, the colour returning to her face as she checked each one off on a finger.

The waiter reappeared with plates of pasta, strands slick with olive oil and butter, flecks of green parsley and cracked black pepper. I bit down on something small and garlicky. It felt like muscle.

The moment my mouth was full, Harry took charge of the conversation. His eyes flashed as he talked about his business, rugby, the irritating lefties at the Front Line Club. He used the phrase 'sexually pleasant' about his colleague's wife. He talked about the problem of labour unions, his roofing contractor, the poetry of Frank O'Hara, his father's summer house in Denmark, before landing on the subject of Joanna's family estate. He was at once exasperated, then passionate. Boisterous then whimsical. Shreds of parsley gathered between those white, white teeth.

I let the words wash over me as I watched Joanna twirl her spaghetti.

Suddenly, cool skin against mine. Joanna clasped my hand beneath the table and held it tight. I grinned.

As Harry continued, I began to understand the enormity of Joanna's wealth. She had grown up in a house on Eton Square, a grand address in Belgravia with a white stucco facade and manicured gardens. I knew from the papers it was London's richest postcode. Past prime ministers, Dutch royalty and Hollywood stars had all lived there.

Joanna squeezed my thumb. The beginnings of a flush spread across my neck.

If Harry noticed his wife leaning away from him, her arm stretching beneath the table, he gave no sign. Or rather he did not let up. On and on went his running commentary on Joanna's breeding, like a horse fanatic enthusing about a filly's potential. I already wanted to fuck his wife; I didn't need her net worth to sweeten the deal. But I had to admire his confidence, his energetic way of talking. It was a kind of magnetism.

I released my thumb and gently turned over Joanna's hand so that the fleshy part of her palm was exposed. Lightly, slowly, I stroked it with my middle finger.

Now Harry was talking about her finishing school in

Switzerland, how many languages she spoke, her debutante ball. He mentioned a younger brother but at his name, Joanna snapped back her hand and changed the subject. Harry stroked her neck, something unspoken passing between them, and then ordered two tiramisus, one for me, one for him.

When they arrived, Joanna just smoked and smoked as we spooned the creamy mess, licking our lips and swigging from the brandy balloons which had appeared with dessert. Harry's portion was gone in three mouthfuls and he disappeared to the bathroom so quickly I knew he'd been counting the minutes until the food was over.

There was a rim of cocoa powder left on my plate and I scraped it into a paste, determined to eat every morsel. All this food and drink had only served to increase my appetite. The cocoa powder left a dry fur on my teeth and I ran my tongue over them, thinking about Joanna's mouth as she finally began to talk, her tongue pink and wet behind glossy lips, dancing around her own teeth.

When she fell silent, I realised I'd missed everything she'd said about her children. Maybe it wasn't because I was thinking about her mouth. Maybe it was impossible for me to imagine this woman as a mother. Strung out and wired, milky and tender. Or cruel, like my own.

Harry returned from the bathroom, his eyes tiny pinpricks. He grinned and passed the cocaine under the table, his hand where Joanna's had been moments before. I pointed at his teeth, unable to hold it in any longer. 'Are those real?'

He threw back his head and roared. 'Veneers. They're new. No one else has dared mention them yet.'

He gnashed his teeth and roared like a lion. Heads swivelled in our direction and then looked away again.

'Can you bite an apple with veneers?' I asked, and as Harry guffawed again, Joanna put a hand on my thigh. I held my breath as her fingers slipped upwards. Upwards. So expert.

When I woke this morning I had the taste of honey-dipped apples in my mouth. In my dream, it was Rosh Hashanah and I couldn't remember my mother's name. Now her name is on a sign outside a prayer room, her birth and death date in small numbers beneath.

'We're early,' Arnold whispers.

But Simone shakes her head. We're not early. She was right: the room is close to empty. A woman I'm told was our mother's cleaner and another assumed to be her daughter, four of Simone's childhood friends, only two of which have come with their husbands. I was bracing myself to see at least one of the women from Carlton Mansions. But no. Maybe there is no one left.

This means there will not be enough men for the minyan at the shiva. Where to find another eight to recite the Kaddish and make our mother's death official in the eyes of her god? It is important to my sister to uphold this tradition, to do her duty.

We walk to our seats closest to the coffin. Plain polished

wood, a small Magen David in its centre. I don't know where to look. I feel eyes on me.

Joanna packed two options for me today: one of her sensible black trouser suits and silk shirts I could just squeeze into, or my black leather trousers, matching jacket, and a black cashmere sweater. I walked downstairs, bracing myself for a reaction. Arnold appeared amused then resumed eating his cornflakes. Simone simply asked if I had slept well. I wonder what so much composure costs her.

My leathers creak as I try to get comfortable. The prayer hall is simple. High ceiling, red brick, long elegant panes of glass on either side. It smells damp. The coffin is both at the front and in the middle of the room, so that we are almost sitting around it. I adjust my trousers, glancing sideways at Simone. Quietly, she says, 'I'm not going to get mad about your leathers. You forget I lived with her longer than you. I couldn't let anything rattle me in that household or I wouldn't have survived. I'm not starting now. It's just clothes.'

'Fair enough,' I whisper. We smile.

Her friends move two rows to sit behind us so that we form a cluster. The rabbi arrives. He greets Simone and Arnold and then introduces himself. I shake his rough, dry hand. He tells me he is sorry for my loss and then turns to my sister and says, 'My dear, someone has sent flowers.'

'Flowers?' Simone asks. 'Who would do that?'

He whispers Joanna's name and my cheeks flame. She has tried to be thoughtful but there are no flowers at a Jewish funeral, no pretty stems, their life cycle snipped short. Mourning is too solemn for decoration. Respects should be paid in person by attending the damn funeral, by sitting shiva. Or with food at least. A sandwich platter would have been more appropriate.

Simone tells the rabbi to give them to the cemetery staff. He nods and goes to the stand where his prayer book lies open.

She turns to me. 'It was a nice gesture.'

Perhaps a nice gesture, perhaps a provocative kindness – just like her choice of clothing. 'She doesn't know . . .' I say.

Rather than ask why Joanna isn't here, Simone explains that the rabbi found some volunteers from the synagogue for the minyan. I am relieved for my sister. I am devasted she has to rely on compassion.

I wonder when the rabbi will give up and realise no one else is coming. At least the quiet is a comfort. I couldn't have stomached sobbing, couldn't have dealt with breathy sorrow. I'm glad Anais went to school today.

'This must be a terrible shock for you, Edie,' a voice says. I turn. It belongs to one of Simone's friends. I'm surprised she knows my name.

Simone looks at us and I can see that she's thinking, *Why? By what right?*

I thank the friend, though her concern is misplaced. My mother and I said our not-so-fond farewells a long time ago. People think the worst thing is for a mother to outlive her children. It is the correct way round for us to be here and for her to be in that coffin. But since I've been dead to her for so long, I'm not so sure if I have outlived her. A conundrum. Besides, there is no one here from the past to say how glad they are to see both her children. No prodigal return without a witness.

The rabbi gives up waiting and speaks a few customary prayers in Hebrew, voice low and heavy with occasion. He returns to English for the *hespeid*. I cross and uncross my legs, then lean forward. It will take a stranger for me to hear facts about my mother's life. Simone does not like to discuss the past, so what little I know came from my mother's lips and since she was prone to hyperbole of epic proportions the truth of those stories is uncertain. Her anecdotes, whether about family, or what she ate for breakfast, had so many holes, so many rearrangements. Even her age changed. Older than most new brides when she met my father, she was creative with her personal timeline. It wouldn't surprise me to discover her last birthday was eighty-five rather than eighty.

'Zelda was born in Odessa,' the rabbi says. 'Daughter of Sonya and Maxim. Her family, who had survived earlier pogroms by going into hiding with relatives in the countryside, returned to the city in a brief period of peacetime where Zelda was born. Here they ran a dress shop with Sonya's sister, Gitlya, until she left the city and settled in Stamford Hill just before the outbreak of the Second World War. The rest of the family stayed on until the siege of Odessa which took the life of Maxim and Zelda's young husband. Sonya and Zelda fled and joined Gitlya in Stamford Hill.'

I blink. My mother was married before she met my father? I turn to Simone to see if she knows, but of course she does: she supplied the details of our mother's life to the rabbi.

In a daze, I miss the rest of what he says. I catch something about her love of shopping.

'I'll end with a short reading from Rabbi Sheila Shulman,' the rabbi says.

With that, I come to. Sheila Shulman, the feminist, lesbian rabbi. Hailing from Brooklyn, now living in London, I've followed her with pleasure from afar. I have no idea why this rabbi is reading from her work. A small smile flickers on Simone's lips.

'We recognise,' the rabbi says, 'that each of us is not so much a person as a world, or rather, the bearer, in her or his self, of a world – a unique, irreplaceable, populated world, linked by myriad threads to other such worlds, and that if, when, someone dies who has been a part of our life, there is a rent in the universe, like a star vanishing, but that like a star vanishing, that world leaves ineradicable traces in us as a star does in space. So that we mourn, but we remember . . . and we know that there will be a living trace of that person in our consciousness always.'

Shulman has the last word. The whole service is over in fifteen minutes.

My mother's cleaner loudly whispers to her daughter, 'Is the family not going to speak?'

My sister does not go in for performance. And what I have to say is best left unsaid.

We turn to leave the prayer hall and that's when I see Kiki, standing by the door. She raises a hand, inclines her head.

'Who is that?' Simone whispers.

'Joanna's daughter. I've no idea why she's here.'

Simone squints and I can tell she's trying to find echoes of Joanna's face in her daughter but there is none. Stella got her mother's genes. 'The more the merrier?' Simone says. 'Can she recite Kaddish?'

I wonder if this is a slight on Kiki, a taking-down of the masculine suit she's wearing. Her lips are purple, eyelids mauve and rimmed with kohl. She looks as out of place as me – more, even. I go over and say, 'I didn't know I'd invited Marc Bolan.'

She laughs and then hushes herself. I hug her. When I pull back, she stares at my leathers. 'I drove here on the Harley,' she says. 'It's like you knew.'

'How did *you* know about all this?' I ask. A pathetic way to describe my mother's funeral.

'Mummy,' she said. 'I couldn't believe she wasn't coming – I mean . . . I came in her place.'

'Clearly they don't work you hard enough at art school.' What I should have said is *thank you*, but the words stick in my throat.

'They don't work me at all.' She smiles.

Some men from the synagogue pick up the coffin in a rehearsed sequence. We leave the prayer hall, trailing behind everyone else.

'She really killed herself?' Kiki asks in a whisper.

'She really did.'

'That is fucking heavy.'

Outside, the others are washing their hands in a small basin. Kiki asks why and I explain it's customary to wash your hands after a funeral and then let them air dry to show you're not eager to wipe away thoughts of loss and mourning. I don't join them at the basin.

We make our way to the graveside. No sun, the sky still so grey. The grounds are carefully maintained, grass cut short, gravel paths free of mud. The headstones have taken on a silvery quality in the frost. A relatively new cemetery, it's peaceful here. Uncrowded. My mother won't have to share her resting place after all.

I reflect on my sister's request to stay the week and help sort our mother's belongings, to go beyond this perfunctory ritual and make myself useful. It wouldn't be so bad to spend a few more nights in Simone's spare room. Hers is a true family home – well managed and warm. A space that holds the people she loves. Perhaps it would be nice to read a bedtime story with Anais. Make a stew one evening for dinner. But to stay also means walking through the door of Carlton Mansions again.

The alternative: Joanna's body stretched across her side of our bed. The sweet chaos of the dogs, their wet noses. The enormity of Damson Manor and its noisy silence. The despair of long days. Cleaning.

It feels impossible to say yes or to say no.

The coffin arrives at the empty grave. Two men I assume to be from the synagogue join us. They stand back respectfully, murmuring the final Hebrew prayers, the words of which come to me from memory, forming themselves automatically. I watch my sister's face, waiting for some emotion to show. But nothing. It's over.

As bodies shift and turn away from the grave, one of the men asks my sister if she has given thought to the stone setting which will take place in six months' time. He wants to let her know there is a good maintenance care programme here. We can join it. Twice-yearly inspections will check that time and nature have not damaged the memorial. Twice-yearly cleaning will be carried out to remove the dirt, algae and lichen that can stain and damage an untended stone.

This dying business, such a business. Such expense.

I intervene, tell the man my sister will make these decisions in due course. I sound like Joanna. It is convincing enough for him to murmur his condolences again and turn away.

'I was thinking red,' Simone says, 'for the tombstone. *Missed by the shopkeepers of Brent Cross.*'

I gasp and Simone snorts and then we shake with silent laughter. I draw a breath and say, 'I'll stay the week.'

Simone kisses my cheek and then she goes to speak with her friends. I wonder what I've got myself into.

'What happens next?' Kiki asks, appearing at my side.

'The shiva. Food. Prayers. More people will turn up. It's going to be horrible.'

'So don't go.'

I laugh.

'No really, don't go. Fuck it. Enough of death. Come to my studio. Let's create instead.'

I stare at Kiki, blinking. I can see the plates of uneaten challah egg rolls, hear the polite conversation and louder still all the questions no one dares to ask: why did she kill herself? She had another daughter? *Oy gevalt*, she's *gay?*

I tell Simone that Kiki will drive me back for the shiva. I explain that I can't resist getting on a Harley. She shrugs and warns me to be careful. It's that easy.

Kiki's Harley is parked at the edge of the lot. All black with minimalist chrome, it is low, lean and tough-looking. I've admired it in our driveway but have never ridden with Kiki before.

She hands me a spare helmet and I slide onto the back of the low saddle. 'Hold tight,' she says, and I wrap my arms around her tiny waist, my pelvis tilted against her buttocks. A kick and then a terrible guttural rumble and within seconds we are screaming down back roads. I cling to Kiki, the cold blasting my body, finding its way between the leathers.

Finally, a sensation matching the barely-there feeling I've had for days. Finally, a sound that can drown out my mother's ghost.

The question hadn't been asked so I wasn't sure what I'd said yes to. It was always like that with Joanna and Harry. Like someone had turned a lamp on above my head and asked me to step into the spotlight and suddenly I was unable to see beyond my own feet.

Another expensive dinner, then drinks at Harry's Knightsbridge flat where he stayed when working in the city. It was the first time I'd been invited back.

I was more aware of Harry's body, Harry's smell, than I was of Joanna. His cologne and tobacco, his domain of old leather and velvet, a vase of lilies on the mantlepiece, their blooms broken open, petals threatening to fall. It produced a tightening in my throat which made it hard to swallow.

Joanna moved around the living room, switching on lamps. Harry picked through a pile of records. I felt small, inert.

I went to the window, watched a few people meandering below, tried to focus the blurry colours of the street. It was almost summer but it had started raining, the sky black with a swollen grey belly. I tapped the glass pane. Joanna touched my shoulders, slid off my jacket. 'Get comfortable, darling,' she said. My whole body turned electric.

'You've got to hear this.' Harry was brandishing an Isaac Hayes record. He looked pleased with himself and slipped off the sleeve, bending over the turntable. Joanna emerged from the kitchen, peeling foil from a bottle of Bollinger. My eyes flicked between her and Harry. I couldn't figure out who was driving this.

'Sit, Edie,' she said.

I crossed my legs on the couch. The synth and strings of Hayes's cover of 'Walk On By' crashed into the room. Joanna began to sway her hips. Harry pulled out a silver card holder and knelt beside the glass coffee table. He tipped out the powder and cut it into one long line, then three. A cork popped. Joanna handed me a champagne coupe and sat beside me. Three cats waiting for cream.

Soon: violins swelling alongside the insistent beat, my own thumping heart, Hayes's low voice, everyone smiling. And then Joanna's face appeared in front of mine. Sweet, champagne breath.

She crawled onto my lap and I grasped her tiny waist, afraid she'd change her mind. But Joanna continued to sway as the guitar made its grand entrance, fuzzy tone cutting through layers of melody. I brushed the fringe out of her eyes. Kissed the bridge of her nose. My thumb found her bottom lip, sticky with gloss. There was a pattern to her breathing as she writhed on me. It didn't deviate.

No sharp intake of breath, no unanticipated puff or pant. Her skin was flushed, but she was completely composed. In control. I pulled back.

Joanna smiled and then looked over her shoulder. There was Harry in a red leather armchair, watching, white veneers flashing. Blood rushed into my ears. And then I saw it: the flat's red curtains, red cushions, deep burgundy carpet. I was suddenly back in Carlton Mansions, back in my mother's world.

I closed my eyes and concentrated on imagining other colours. Baskets of pink summer peaches; an indigo ink stain flowering across a finger. When I opened them again Joanna was out of her cape, lace bra against tanned skin. She was even thinner than I had expected, her expression still relaxed, full of unhurried energy. I slid her closer until we were rocking together and then I tipped her head back, kissed her throat.

'Bedroom,' Harry commanded.

I followed Joanna.

I took off my clothes and then I took off Joanna's lingerie. A blonde mass of pubic hair soft against her concave stomach. The endpoints of her body fascinated me. The peaks of her nipples, hip bones, the polished curve of her toenails. I made my way around her body. Her skin shone with sweat.

Harry sat on the edge of the bed, drinking champagne, silent, his gaze trained on Joanna like he was taking in the image of a stranger. And then I saw the three of us clearly. Through me, Harry was going to discover Joanna all over again. Fall in love again. My body was an instrument, a conduit for something much more private, more personal, between them.

I hesitated, but too late – there was her mouth, seeking. Teasing.

I did not know how much Joanna was performing, or if she was performing at all. I did not know if this softer face was her truer face, or something she had arranged to please me. I desired her too much to care. Enough to ignore our audience. I had become so good at ignoring whatsoever it pleased me to ignore.

I closed my eyes, gave in to pleasure. The record ended and the needle clicked alongside my moans. I clenched my thighs tight, guiding the sensations. But I could feel Harry watching. White teeth glinting in the dark. My eyes flicked open. He'd moved from the bed to an armchair. I relaxed. He wasn't going to touch me. That was not what he wanted. He was letting Joanna sate herself.

Was this devotion?

There were her fingers – confident, controlled. So much control. And as she traced tiny circles on my clit, my body began to thrill under the impact of their joint gaze. I found myself responding to it. Now I was the one who was performing.

When I came for the second time, Harry ejaculated right onto the carpet. He left the mess there for the cleaner in the morning.

I should be at my mother's shiva, in Simone's clean home. Instead, I'm at Kiki's Piccadilly studio, muscles cramping as I lie prone on her tiny couch. A weak sun pushes a creamy light through the leaded windows. The walls are splashed with moments of accidental colour. Canvases crowd the corners.

'Is that why you haven't seen your sister?' Kiki asks.

She's rolled up the sleeves of her shirt, plucked its length from the waistband of her trousers. Now it reaches her knees, swamping her petite frame. She squints, paintbrush in hand, a large canvas stretched across the easel in front of her. A boiled sweet clanks against her teeth.

'Edie?' Kiki looks up. It's so cold I can see her breath.

I take a deep breath, inhaling the resinous oils and turps. It's natural for Kiki to be curious after meeting my sister for the first time. Perhaps it's easier to talk about this rather than my mother's funeral, a funeral with no real sadness. No shaking shoulders, no blotchy faces, no wailing. I am a little embarrassed by the utter lack of drama. Most funerals elevate the deceased to sainthood – if only for the time it takes to speak their eulogy. Yet not one kind word was spoken about my mother.

'Simone visited the house once,' I say, 'just after she got married. You and Stella were very young and away at school. It didn't go well. In those days the house was like a—'

'I know,' Kiki snaps. 'We'd find things. It was our horrible sex education.' Her cheeks flame. 'Honestly, Edie. Do you really think it all went over our heads? She glares at the canvas. 'You were a splinter in our lives.'

I swallow. It's been a long time since Kiki's temper has surfaced. Her childhood tantrums were so furious she'd vomit on herself. Not that I had witnessed many, too caught up in my own pleasure. Back then, my mind was at ease as long as my appetites were satiated, though perhaps this is true for everyone. I allowed myself uppers, wine to come down. Sex to stay alert, to disappear, to drowse through the days. I thought I was at my most free. It took too long to realise I was only arranging my own internment at the house. With a pulse of shame, I realise I don't even remember the first time I met Kiki.

I murmur her name.

Her eyes flash, brows raise. 'We weren't exactly a normal family, were we? No matter how Mummy used to spin it. Stella and I arrived home from boarding one summer and there you were – living in the coach house. A "friend of the family" we'd never met before, who went more places with our parents than we ever did, and who never left.' She lets out a sigh. 'We didn't have the word for it yet, but you couldn't have looked more like a dyke back then if you'd tried. We thought you were an alien.'

She suddenly bursts into laughter. 'I'm sorry, I shouldn't have called you a splinter. But it was exactly like that. A sharp, almost brilliant pain. And then, after a while, the pain dulls. You become used to it, stop noticing. But lately, it's like I've pulled out that splinter. I feel . . . lighter. Less angry.' Kiki blinks a few times. 'You've stiffened,' she says. 'Relax.'

I drop my shoulders though I can't believe she expects me not to be rattled. She's never spoken to me so directly before.

We sit in silence. It goes on.

Finally, Kiki starts talking again, addressing the canvas. She tells me that for as long as she can remember, she's been interested in how other people tell their family stories. What they choose to reveal, what remains hidden. It doesn't take a shrink to figure out why. Over the years, she continues, that interest has taken different forms, lots of phases. She's drawn to anything that allows its maker to tell their story. *Little obsessions*, Joanna calls them. Manga, films, dance, poetry, music. 'Mummy thinks I'll drop painting as soon as something shiny turns my head.' Kiki pauses, laughs, but it is a bitter sound. 'I guess that's also why she can't take my romantic relationships seriously. I can't blame her.'

She turns to look at me. 'You asked before why I'm so interested in installations and video when I study fine art,' she says, 'and I've been thinking more about that. There's something so direct about video. It draws all my interests together. Words, movement, cinematography. And it stays with me in a way a painting doesn't or can't. It haunts me.'

She looks back at the canvas and begins to tell me about a short film by the artist Patty Chang. Wearing a white bustier and balancing a plate on her head, Chang tells the story of her aunt's death from breast cancer. While talking, she slices through the fabric of her bra with an enormous carving knife. Inside is a honeydew melon. She scoops out the fruit's seeds with her fingers and piles it on the plate.

Kiki stops. I'm never sure how she wants me to respond to these art lessons. I tell her to continue.

'Chang is doing too much at once,' she says, 'and she struggles. It's a balancing act but she manages to keep her entire body motionless except for the arm that slices the fruit. The scene is static, very still, but it's also explosive. Horrifying to watch. And as Chang spoons the flesh of the melon into her mouth, you can't help but feel like she's eating her own breast. Devouring her story even as she tells it.'

My mouth suddenly fills with the flavour of my father's tortilla, the sweetness of fried onions. And then in floods my mother's chicken soup, lokshen, dissolving on the tongue. Combined, the flavours are all wrong, each one trying to suppress the other. I want a glass of water but Kiki is painting again, frowning.

'And you?' I dare to ask. 'What are you trying to say with this portrait?'

She shrugs. 'I'm a novice. I'm just trying to resist blurring the details of your face. You have sharp edges, Edie, packed with grief.' She breaks into a smile. 'Don't look so alarmed. There's as much of me in this as there is you. I'm just as exposed. Think of it as a double-sided page; my description of you is my description of me.'

'How terrifying,' I say.

Kiki steps away from the canvas. Circles it. Frowns. We are quiet for a while. She puts down the palette, walks to the sink, returns with a new brush and then scrapes something from the page.

I tune in to the hum of the electric heater, watch the sky grow darker through the window behind Kiki's head. And then she says, so quietly I have to strain to hear, 'The truth is, I don't know if I can make this painting any good. I've let you be a stranger to me. You were one more person to get through before I reached Mummy. We didn't need that, Stella and I.'

'I know,' I whisper.

'We hated you.'

'You had every right. I didn't give you any thought.'

'*Mummy* was thoughtless,' Kiki says, gripping the paintbrush tight. 'She still is.'

I want to offer solidarity but I'm afraid of betraying Joanna. She did not try to rummage in my life and rearrange it. She simply offered me an escape route and I took it. It was far easier to exist in her life than in mine. I am in her debt.

'Being with Chloe and Ryan has made me understand

your situation more,' Kiki says. 'I expected it to bring me closer to Mummy, but it did the opposite. It brought me to you.' She lays the paintbrush on the side of the palette.

I unfurl from my position, cross the room, and take a seat on the stool next to her. To my surprise, she is shaking. In a small voice Kiki begins to talk to me about her childhood, a story I thought I knew but as she gathers speed, staring straight ahead, it's like I've been reading with my eyes closed. She tells me that the noise in the house never bothered Stella when they returned from boarding school, but she had terrible insomnia as a child, unable to sleep through the reverberating turntable, the giggling and the shouting. She'd wander among the airless, smoke-clouded rooms that rocked and swayed with bodies and join the party unnoticed. A tiny, elfin child, she took it all in. The ashtrays spilling cigar butts and coloured Gauloises which looked like candy sticks. Crystal glasses patterned with lipstick. The women whose jewellery jangled at their ears and wrists. The men's open shirts, chests curling with hair, gold chains glinting. So much skin. She would look for Joanna, not because she wanted comfort, but because she wanted a glimpse. Her mother was so beautiful at these parties, hair shining, eyelids shimmering, clothed in a dress of silk so sleek it was as if it had been poured onto her body. And when Kiki found her, she'd stand in a doorway and watch her mother dance, all hips and elbows and knees, the knotty, angular parts of her leading, head thrown back, before rushing up to her and winding closely around her legs like a cat, cheek pressed into the back of a sweaty knee. Joanna would tolerate her there for a moment, fixing Kiki's bed-mussed hair, turning her around for everyone to admire, before shooing her back upstairs.

She looks at me. 'You'd be in a corner somewhere, with that huge mop of black curls, wearing a waistcoat and smoking one of Daddy's cigars, fondling some woman's oversized earring.'

My heart sinks.

'I never saw you with Mummy at their parties,' she says.

'Joanna was the hostess. Busy pleasing everybody.'

Kiki inhales sharply and then begins speaking again. She remembers one particular summer night, when she was eight or nine years old, when the combination of heat and noise was so terrible she couldn't lie still a second longer. Stella, who had been tasked with keeping Kiki in their bedroom at night, was fast asleep. Emboldened by her need for a glass of water, she tiptoed out and along the corridor and down the stairs.

The party was winding down and the remaining guests were flopped across couches, glasses tinkling with ice as they drank and talked. To get to the kitchen, she had to pass the ground-floor guest bedroom and there a strange noise stopped her at the door. At first, what she saw was only in the abstract. A blur of shapes. Pink and brown splodges. Pain sounds. The smell of a gymnastics lesson. Her mind worked to put all the pieces together but there were only seeds of understanding. She rushed back to her room where her sister was still sleeping and stood by the open window, gulping fresh air, keeping her eyes on the moon as she looked out across the otherwise dark gardens.

'I feel', she says quietly, 'that night awoke something quite dangerous in me.'

And then I realise what she has been describing because I have seen it, too. Joanna's naked body on all fours, Harry's cock in her mouth, penetrated from behind by a stranger.

Saliva floods my gums. My tongue, thick and too large, sticks in my throat.

But Kiki isn't done yet. As she continues, Harry appears in her story as gruff and rambunctious and an obvious drunk. Joanna is so cold that she only warms in the arms of strangers, and I say, 'Stop, please. I can't. I can't.' I cannot stand the unspoken accusation that I was an accomplice to all that pain.

I put my head in my hands and remember the house as it was to me back then, a place of immediate luxury, the freedom to follow desire, to follow all sensory pleasure, of time untethered. Kiki and Stella were both there and not there, the two bedroom doors emblazoned with their names pulled shut most of the year. Of course, I knew they were part of the family. They briefly appeared between school terms before they were packed off to day camps, relatives, horse-riding lessons, ballet classes. I'd never given thought to the occasions they might have been exposed to parties. In my mind those bedroom doors had stayed shut, the contents frozen in time, all pink and peach and pretty. Untouched. I had not considered they might simply turn the handle and walk out into our world, big blue eyes blinking.

And yet. Kiki had seen it. She had seen it all.

Kiki takes my hand, squeezes, even though it is me who should be doing the comforting. 'It's not on you,' she says. 'It predates you. They were always that way, I think. I don't know. I've never had the courage to ask.'

I try to steady my breathing. 'I feel as if I'm dissolving,' I murmur.

She drops my hand and turns back to her easel. Kiki has snapped back from the past. She considers the painting. 'I really need you to not dissolve. I need you to firm up, actually. Become more real. I thought your face was so familiar to me but it's not. I'm trying to find it.' She sighs and tells me she wasn't exaggerating when she said the image would be as much about her as it was about me. 'But I've tipped the balance,' she says. 'I always tip the balance. My tutor was right. I can't see women for what they are. I centre myself in everything.'

'Then it's a collaboration. What's wrong with that?' I ask. 'The video you just described was a collaboration between the artist and her aunt. Is this not the same? A collaboration between two women? Three, if we count your mother?'

'Mummy is not a collaborator. She's a dictator.'

I smile and Kiki looks away and out through the window. The sky is fully dark and I wonder, loosely, about the time. It passes so differently in the studio.

'When were you last in a bar?' she asks.

'A bar?'

'Or a club?'

I confess I haven't a clue.

'Let's get out of here then,' she says.

'Don't you want to continue?'

She shakes her head. 'Not today.'

I find myself following Kiki through Soho as it pulses around us. And it's not as if I've forgotten my mother's shiva is in full swing – I can well imagine the version of myself sitting beside Simone, quietened, dampened – it's just I'm glad not to be her.

The bar is at the end of a cobbled side street. A bouncer nods us through the door. I pause at the entrance. The majority of the room is a dance floor, high tables and stools arranged around its edges, banquettes beneath the shuttered windows. It is so much busier than I'd anticipated, so many bodies bathed in blue light.

Kiki laughs in my ear. 'Your eyes are wide!'

I tell her I'm remembering what it feels like to be in a room entirely full of women. It is fucking glorious.

Kiki grins, then unbuttons her shirt and ties it around her waist, revealing a flat belly and a white cotton crop top. I slip off my leather jacket, then Joanna's jumper, until I'm just in a vest and then Kiki takes my hand and we snake through the crowd on the dance floor to the bar.

'I'm buying,' she shouts over the music, all bass, all beat, and orders two vodka tonics. Sucking through the straw, thirst awakened, I find I've swallowed most of the drink in one go. Kiki laughs again. Her eyes are lively and I can tell she is amused to see me here, in her world – a version of which was once mine.

'Want to dance?' she asks, but I don't know how to move to this music so I order another drink while Kiki finds her friends on the dance floor. She disappears into the knot of bodies. Writhing, undulating. I lean my back against the bar.

A lone dancer on the edge of the crowd catches my eye with her shaved, bleached head. The lines of her firm buttocks ripple through her lime green cycling shorts, abs contracting beneath a tiny bralette. There is so much control in her limbs, each movement alive with intention. Not swept away by the music but part of it. Sweat runs between her sharp shoulder blades, trickles into the small of her back. Her skin shines. My eyes wander over the definition of her collar bone, the tiniest breasts pushing against cotton. I swallow another mouthful of my drink and move along the bar.

Closer, I can see she must be about forty. How I would like to press myself against that muscular body. Slide a thumb into the damp groove of her neck. I allow myself to imagine her lips on mine. Plump and moist. The insistent force of her tongue as it fills my mouth. I pluck the lime from my glass and bite into its sharp flesh. I work the fruit away from the rind and my body floods with energy. I am gently sucking on her swollen labia, pulling the lips a little with my teeth.

She knows I'm watching and keeps dancing. There is

so much joy in her body. She smiles. I smile back and it's hard to catch my breath. And then there is a firm hand around my wrist, dragging me onto the dance floor. 'Come on,' Kiki says. 'Chloe's here and she wants to meet you.' I let myself be carried along, be absorbed into the crowd, and I think back to the artist slicing the melon nestled in her bra and wonder: what did she do with all those scooped-out seeds?

I hope they were planted, allowed to grow. But what would they become? Fruit or bra?

I left my bedsit without paying the last month's rent. It didn't take long to pack. A driver picked me up from London. It was so hot that summer that I gave in to sluggishness and slept through the journey. When I woke, my back was stuck to the leather. By the look on the driver's face, I'd been snoring.

I arrived at Damson Manor with very little, unsure how long I wanted to stay, unsure how long I was welcome. It was the weekend and party preparations were already underway. Stupidly, I thought it was in my honour. When we pulled into the drive, I couldn't believe two people called this place home. I'd already forgotten the children lived there, too. Joanna told me they spent most of the summer in Denmark with Harry's parents.

The coach house was set to the left of the main house. The driver let me out and told me the key was under the mat. He turned the car around and headed to Broadstairs station to pick up other party guests.

Joanna rushed out of the front door as the car pulled away.

'You're here!' she said and kissed me on the mouth. Her gold earrings swung against my neck. She was already dressed for the night. She looked perfect. She always looked perfect.

I took a long, cool bath with oils from tiny glass bottles arranged on the side of the tub, dressed in my favourite flares and white vest and then joined the party.

By now, no spoils of old money could surprise me. In fact, I'd thought there would be more opulence – the party was like any London society party except the house was much larger and more remote and consequently made the people seem smaller. To compensate, there were lots of guests and the lights were dimmed with orange bulbs so it felt like we were sloshing around in a patchouli-scented womb together, our feet sinking into shagpile. Art dealers and lawyers, bankers and musicians – they were all there. The one thing they had in common? Money.

It took four vodka martinis before it dawned on me that there were also many rooms to stay in overnight. The party did not have to stop after one evening. It could go on for days in comfort.

Outside, the garden shone with strings of lights and the surface of the swimming pool glimmered. I danced with Joanna just once before I lost her to the crowd. She was a consummate hostess. All pleasantries and flirtation. When the plates of drugs came out, they were displayed on freestanding silver wine coolers. The party grew louder. Guffaws mixed with conversation about summer homes and Nepalese spices. I felt sick. Did two lines to sober up while talking to a journalist. Her thick lashes caressed the tops of her cheeks as she spoke about Germaine Greer. I did another line so I could follow her argument. And then, as pairs of couples slunk away, I saw what made these parties different from the ones I'd been to with my friend Annie and her set.

The rules of an ordinary home did not appear to apply here. If a home was supposed to protect the people inside and keep strangers out, what was this house?

I let the journalist kiss me and I let her husband watch. The feeling of eyes on me had become its own drug, too exhilarating not to embrace. I declined the invitation to their bedroom. It would take me much longer to fully inhabit that role.

In the space between parties, Damson Manor became the most peaceful place I'd ever known. Harry spent the week managing his business in the city. The children visited and then returned to boarding school, my presence explained as a family friend. I couldn't believe how simple it all was. I had no need to work, forgot about setting an alarm. I signed on for benefits to cover my few outgoings.

The coach house was larger than anywhere I'd lived before. It had good light and the back looked out over the enormous grounds which were full of flowering bushes and lawns with perfect stripes. Everywhere smelled of jasmine. It was silent, which is to say it took me a good while to realise all I could hear was birdsong. In London there were too many competing sounds: ice cream vans, human agitation, the way building never stops. Later, I wondered if I'd just been carrying those noises in my head like an unending car alarm. Like my mother's voice.

Hundreds of paperbacks filled the shelves and I made my way through them, unselectively, languorously. *Madame Bovary. The Second Sex. In Search of Lost Time.* Many classics I'd read before, many I hadn't. I allowed each one to change my life in its own way, just as when I'd read Syd's copy of *The Well of Loneliness*. I avoided contemporary novels if I could help it. I didn't want reminders of the outside world. I found I couldn't stomach poetry.

I had no friends in Broadstairs and no one from my old life came to visit. Annie went to rehab and when she came out, she moved away, cut ties. I read for hours, completely immersed. I lived with those characters and their worlds as much as I did with Joanna. She spent her time exercising, at the hairdresser, beauticians, lunching with friends. Sometimes I joined her, but these occasions made me feel like her pet. In fact, she had started calling me Poodle, affectionately so she said, after my mass of dark curly hair. Not that she used that name in front of anyone else. She wasn't cruel. And because I had no name for what we were, for what I was to Joanna, I remained silent. I remained silent for a long time.

That first summer, the two of us fell into an easy rhythm. I loved the dogs immediately. Only when Harry returned at the weekends did I feel like an outsider. He was welcoming and generous but he was also protective. Not in a jealous way, or at least he wasn't sexually jealous. He was protective of his empire, as he called it. He made it clear what belonged to him, a terrain that was impossibly vast in my eyes, extending from his family history to his business, to his great big house and his beautiful wife and daughters. Men and their legacy. I didn't have the stomach for that either.

But Harry's ego was a small price to pay. Until now, I hadn't realised the extent of my exhaustion. In the city I'd been focused on climbing. I'd glimpsed how other people lived and wanted it. I'd slipped into a milieu where I dressed so much like an interloper I wasn't considered one. The truth was, I liked luxury. Plush fabric, high ceilings, single malt whiskeys. French food, fast cars, watches that hung heavy on the wrist. Most of all I liked ease. The end to mental calculations at the grocer's or shimmying out the back window when the landlord knocked. I hung up my hustle with aplomb.

When the high season ended, Joanna took me to the beach. I was stunned. I'd only ever seen the sea in Brighton during summertime and there it was as noisy and chaotic as the city. In the diffused September light, Broadstairs was different. Calmer, yet the cliffs made the scene majestic. The dogs ran and ran, raced into the water, shook themselves off and then started the whole cycle again.

It was still warm enough to sit out. We'd brought a seafood picnic and two crusty baguettes. Joanna slipped off her linen shirt, revealing a gold bikini beneath. I dipped prawns in a pot of mayonnaise. She spread crab pate thickly, opened a bottle of Chablis. We ate and watched the dogs play.

I stretched out my legs, dug my toes in the sand. 'There's nothing nicer than a full stomach and the feeling of warm sun on your body,' I said. 'Why is that?'

She drained her wine. 'Wittgenstein said, "What you say, you say in a body; you can say nothing outside of this body." I think about that often,' she said. 'Then again, Wittgenstein was thinking about *his* body, the male body.' She bit into a prawn. 'He was against women having the vote, you know.'

Joanna's eyes were hidden behind enormous sunglasses. Teasing, I said, 'Doesn't it bother you that you have all this education and no use for it?'

'Darling,' she said, smiling, 'I used my education to seduce *you*, didn't I?'

She would have kissed me then but there were too many people on the beach. Instead, she lay back, stretched her body, her wonderful body. 'I like having you around, Edie,' she said to the sky.

It was enough for me.

Simone parks the car and then my feet are on Elgin Avenue again. Three decades and yet how unchanged it all is. The red phone box still there on the corner, the cord loose and dangling. The familiar sound of children's cries carries from the recreation ground. Only the oak trees seem smaller, though I know this cannot be true, and the buildings are cleaner, more impressive than I remember. There is money here now.

It is a beautiful morning, crisp but bright, the kind of winter day longed for after a lengthy stretch of grey. I take a deep breath in and my exhale fogs the air. 'There she is,' I say to Simone, though she's too far away to hear me. Carlton Mansions' red brick glows beneath the sun.

The keys jangle in Simone's hand and in the other is a Thermos of hot tea and a packed lunch. She visibly steels herself as we climb the steps to the shared front door. Last time she was here, our mother's body lay waiting. I put a hand on Simone's shoulder. She turns and nods and we take the stairs to the third floor. I balance two cardboard boxes filled with black rubbish bags. Keep. Sell. Charity shop. We come prepared. We have a method.

I've been forgiven for disappearing after the funeral, for missing shiva, for staying out like a naughty child and waking up Anais to get in. Years of enduring our mother has made Simone unbearably reasonable. But I suspect it was also easier not to have me there. The lost daughter. The shame. The spectacle. No curious strangers, no explanation necessary. Better to stay lost.

The corridor has been painted recently. There's a lingering smell, astringent and hopeful. The prices in this building have rocketed. Yet the bones of Carlton Mansions remain unchanged and I find myself caught between two moments in time, rocked with inertia.

Simone opens the flat door. It's dark inside, curtains drawn, slim cracks of daylight bursting through the gaps. There are bags and boxes everywhere. To my right is the old ottoman, letters stacked in a pile. I swallow. Every inch of my body longs to be somewhere else. But I've made a promise.

We both loiter in the hallway.

So often, talk of death drawing near speaks of a sudden chill, a blast of freezing air, hairs standing on end. But it is warm here with a totally different smell to the one I remember. Tangy and sweet. I shift the weight of the box onto my other hip and sniff.

'Microwave meals,' Simone says, staring at our mother's bedroom door. It is closed.

'Really?' I recall my mother's voracious appetite, how

she learned to love food after my father left. The hours spent cooking recipes she remembered from her own mother. My first taste of sorrel soup, knishes and kugels.

'We gave her a microwave one year and that was it. She bought all her meals at Marks & Spencer. Penne arrabbiata was a particular favourite. The only time she ate something fresh was at ours.'

I shrug. So my mother succumbed to convenience. Since she found life to be an unholy struggle, it shouldn't be such a surprise.

I set down the boxes and ask where we should start, and this is when Simone confesses that what lies ahead of us is a mammoth task. She tells me that until last week, she hadn't actually been inside the flat for years. Our mother never let her cross the threshold. She had to wait in the hallway, Arnold in the car. They paid for a cleaner once a week and asked no questions.

I cannot imagine my sister not insisting, but maybe it was one too many battles. 'Well, well,' I say. 'After all those years of being a *baleboste*, she becomes a hoarder. We'll add it to our list of gripes.'

Simone smiles and it is such a relief to see her face relax, I think I can get through this. I gesture at the living room. She springs into action, opening the curtains. Light floods in and I rub my eyes. Everything red. Everything where I last saw it.

'She held on to it all,' Simone says.

The old furniture is here, plus three new sideboards jammed at various angles against the walls, an 80s television, a creaky-looking maroon leather couch. It's not dirty, just stale and lifeless. But no. There's a large black fly buzzing against the sash window. His plump body circles the air and then charges at the glass. Falls. Buzzes. Charges again. He must have been here when my mother died. The only witness. I go to the window and fiddle with the lock until it shifts. Cold rushes in.

'Good idea,' Simone says. With a blue Sharpie, she has already begun to label the cardboard boxes. She suggests starting with the sideboards.

I turn back to the fly who hasn't moved. 'Go on,' I say. 'You're free.' The fly doesn't budge. 'I've opened the window for you. Go on.'

'Goodness' sake, Edie, stop talking to the fly and come and help.'

Simone has opened one of the sideboards to reveal four drawers full of tights. I raise my eyebrows. 'What was she going to do with those? Make a noose?'

She looks at me, the whites of her dark eyes flashing, and then throws back her head and laughs.

I take a seat on the floor beside her and together we work through the contents methodically. Unopened plastic packs crackle as we throw them into the donate box. Loose tights soon fill two black rubbish bags.

An hour passes. We have drunk the tea. Simone and I silently sort and organise. One cabinet is full of sweaters and cardigans, the other trinkets – old candlesticks, half-burned candles, chipped cups and saucers. I don't know what's more horrifying: the sheer number of objects or that they're grouped together in some semblance of order.

The blank screen of the TV reflects the outline of our bodies. Every so often, I raise my head, expecting my mother to be standing there. No mind we buried her yesterday; her image has haunted me for so long, I didn't expect it to stop. But so far – nothing. That judging voice has gone, for now, anyway. The quiet is more than I can bear. I leave Simone in the living room and go to the kitchen to see if I can find the old radio. I close my eyes and hear the sizzle of my father's tortilla, his tremulous singing. I open them again and there is the same round kitchen table where the women of Carlton Mansions gathered to eat cake and play Kalooki.

The old Bush radio has been replaced by an ugly digital one. I unplug it and return, triumphant, to where Simone has started on another cabinet. Its insides are stuffed with brown pill bottles.

'*Oy vey*,' I say. 'What was she doing? Planning to start a pharmacy?'

I plug in the radio but it suddenly feels sacrosanct to switch it on. I stare at Simone and deep down I know there's not a hope my mother thought to leave me anything but her lingering torpor. 'I'm guessing she didn't mention me in the will?' I blurt out.

Simone looks up. She shakes her head.

'But there is,' I sweep my arms, 'so much here to bequeath.'

She snorts.

'Not even a packet of tights? Or an out-of-date bottle of Valium?'

'Well now, those she needed.' Simone smiles again but her eyes are serious. 'We'll sort it out,' she whispers.

I kneel beside her and see she's holding a small stuffed teddy. 'Benny,' she says, introducing us, lifting a paw in hello. But I remember Benny. She will have forgotten he was a present from me when she was born. 'You loved that bear,' I say. 'You used to chew his ears.'

'I can't believe she kept him,' she says, and then, 'How could she stuff him in a drawer like this?' Simone strokes Benny's head. 'When Dad was away and I was a toddler, she'd threaten to leave me here. Said she wanted time alone.'

'Did she ever do it?'

Simone shakes her head. 'I'd lie awake all night terrified that if I slept, she'd be gone in the morning.'

A flash of a memory. A crib. My cries. The ceiling. 'She *did* leave me,' I say. 'When I was a baby. Once a week, she went to the cinema in the afternoon.'

Simone laughs. 'You're joking.' But she can see from my face that I am not joking. I tell her that I read Zelda's diaries when I was a teenager. She frequently left me alone. Something shifts and squirls in me. I feel those old tears now as if they are fresh and press my fingertips to my cheeks, expecting to find them wet.

I close the flat door behind me and sit on the polished parquet floor, breathing deeply. It's incredible, really, how much someone can own – even if they're not of the hoarding persuasion, buying and buying and then storing it all away to be forgotten. I have renewed gratitude for my few possessions.

And yet, despite being surrounded by objects, those rooms have an emptiness to them. They are an arrangement of absences. Young me, my father, now my mother, too. All gone. Fuzzy white spaces where our bodies used to be, like the tampered-with 70s porn video Kiki described, the women nothing but shimmering ghosts. But at Carlton Mansions the men were removed too. My mother managed only, what, thirteen of her eighty years with a man before he walked out the door or died?

The sound of coughing brings me to and then, '*Oy gevalt!* Is it really you?'

I look up and there is Vera.

'Edie,' she says, and then, softly, '*ziskayt.*'

It has been so long since I've been called that term of endearment that immediately tears spring up. Hot and surprising.

She crosses the hall. No longer the middle-aged woman of my memories, Vera is an old lady now, black hair turned silver, an effort to her walk. But her eyes are still dark and shrewd, focused on me in disbelief.

I nod at her, mortified by my tears which did not come even at my mother's funeral.

'We thought we'd never see you again,' she says.

My first impulse is to ask if my mother spoke of me. I know she did not with Simone, but perhaps with Vera there was more understanding between the two women. But her expression tells me no. I have long been dead to her as well.

A year after I moved into the coach house, Joanna asked me to join them in the main wing. Harry was travelling more frequently for work. She said she wanted me closer. My new bedroom wasn't as big but no matter, I was on the inside now.

Those first nights were unbearably hot. Too hot to sleep. Naked, I wandered the corridors until I came to their bedroom and saw the door was ajar. I sat on the carpet and watched both bodies atop the sheets, window open, dawn stirring.

Joanna was on her side facing Harry; he was flat on his back, snoring. She breathed out, murmured, slender body stretching. Pink satin riding up tanned thigh. Her hand sought Harry's belly and then she hooked her arm over its mass. She slid closer, moulding herself to his side, eyes closed. Impossible to tell if she was awake or moving in dreams.

She was still for a moment, then her fingers crept across his skin and caressed the white cotton of his underwear, stroked. He moaned. Coiled around him, she slipped down further until her face was level with his crotch, tongue flicking at the fabric.

I felt his arousal as I watched it grow. Her mouth open and pliant. Gentle sucking sounds. Liquid excitement in my belly.

I put my hand to my own wet slit. Such a thrill to stay silent as I juddered with the force of my climax.

It became a habit, watching them on nights I hadn't been invited to their room. At first, I figured neither Joanna nor Harry was aware of their interloper. They didn't fuck often. I watched them sleeping, snoring, caught the occasional fart. But then I noticed a shift in Joanna's demeanour. A slight arch in her back, elongating her leg, a more pronounced, provocative swish of the hips. It was a performance, I thought, a performance for me. Harry always closed his eyes and she liked to be watched.

We did not speak of what passed between us. It became another form of intimacy that both included and excluded Harry.

Nights passed this way, blurring the edges of our bodies until I could no longer distinguish the sensation of my own desire, so attached was it to theirs.

It was as close as I'd come to happiness. A stable home. I was rooted to the landscape of this quiet part of England and it was those roots that held me during nights that brought other, newer bodies to me, bodies that I didn't know I would enjoy exploring, new ways I didn't know I wanted to have sex. Two, three, four mouths. Two, three, four tastes. My ears echoing with convulsions.

We were telling our stories, I thought, telling them with bodies, not words. Was it so different from the women of Carlton Mansions, how they gathered around the kitchen table unloading themselves, finding comfort and pleasure in shared experience, indulging the senses with the taste of something sweet?

Melting bodily boundaries gave way to a playful, performative version of myself. Sometimes it was a training in pleasure, sometimes it was a training in resilience. Either way, I was getting an education.

Vera's flat is a carbon copy of my mother's except the décor was updated in the 80s. The brown carpet is coarse but spotless, the walls papered in florals. The kitchen smells of lemon cleaner. Vera is still a *baleboste*, still devoted to maintaining a well-run home.

She sits me down at the Formica table, waving away my offer of help, and hands me a teacup and saucer. 'I came to shiva yesterday,' she says, taking the seat opposite. 'You weren't there.'

'You weren't at the funeral.'

We look at each other a moment and then look away. The window frames the bare tops of trees across the recreation ground.

Vera takes a sip of tea. 'And you're helping your sister with Zelda's things?'

I murmur yes and then we fall silent. How to fill in the years? But something softens in Vera and she makes it easy. She tells me of her children, their marriages and their children, their gripes at work. In many ways it is like talking to Simone. Vera has mellowed, as most people do with age or great disappointment – whichever comes first. Her face, however, has stayed defined. No pudding cheeks, her features are drawn and sharp.

Finally, family history exhausted, she spreads her hands wide and says, 'Your mother, she was—'

'Yes,' I say, before she can finish. We smile shyly at each other. 'You know, as a child, I loved her very much,' I say. 'Too much maybe. All I wanted was to be close to her. I loved the smell of her skin. Violet soap. The powdery rose of that Yardley lipstick she always wore.'

Vera reaches across the table and grips my hands. 'You were her firstborn. So longed for.'

I look down and am surprised to see two pairs of old women's hands, loose, lined skin – hers with rings that slip around the knuckles, mine dry and marked with black Sharpie. I look up. The way she holds my gaze, so composed, makes me tremble.

And because I cannot speak about my life, Vera continues. 'Your mother and I were bereaved at the same time. My Dovid, he died in prison. Samuel was hit by a car. We were cursed.' She lets go of my hands. 'And your father? Did you ever find him?'

I shake my head. I never tried. I figured he started again. Somewhere else with someone else, someone easier. Another family. Men are able to do that so easily. 'The men here seemed to evaporate,' I say. 'None of you even gave birth to sons!'

Vera clears her throat. 'It *was* always us women until we – how did you say it? – evaporated too.' Her dark eyes blink hard. 'It happened both fast and slow. One by one we all came down with cancers, the gaps between each one of our diagnoses so small it was like a plague had descended. Rivka first, of course. She never really recovered from what happened. Her mind was . . . Then Dora, hers was sudden at least. Merciful. A year later, Margery. Your mother and I nursed the women best we could until we both got breast cancer. I don't know why we were spared and the others weren't.'

I breathe deeply. Recall Rivka's laugh, her long gold braid.

Vera stands suddenly. 'I forgot the cake,' she says, and turns to open a cupboard. She takes out two white plates and slides a wedge of marble cake onto each one. 'Please,' she says, pushing it towards me, 'it's nice to share something sweet. I made this yesterday.'

The cake is so dry the sponge clags on the roof of my mouth. But Vera seems revived by the sugar, taking large bites. 'We used to think your mother was just sad,' she says in a conspiratorial tone that makes me uneasy. 'There was enough of it to go around. We all held so much sadness in our bodies it's a wonder we could ever stand up straight, let alone walk, be mothers. But *your* mother – she wasn't sad. She was *angry*. She didn't get angry like other people, the way it rises up in them, bursts out, then fades. No, your mother's anger was absolute. A constant. Zelda lived life as if clinging to the sides of a capsizing ship, shouting at the captain for not doing a better job.'

'No,' I say, putting down my fork. 'She *was* the ship. The goddamn *Titanic*. We should have buried her in the

Black Sea, not the suburbs.' And suddenly I am raging against all this loss. 'It didn't have to be that way,' I say, my voice rising. 'Didn't she long for anything beyond being a wife? Didn't she want to get better? To feel *good*?'

I lean back in the chair, exhausted. Vera seems amused and my anger fades. I do not want to imitate my mother. It is not lost on me that that I have become an unwitting wife myself. Had my own imagination not once been full? Had I not hoped for more? What was it that I had desired beyond the lure of a stranger's body?

Vera laughs. 'Forgive me,' she says, 'I'd forgotten. You were so timid when you were small, and then one day – poof – the mouth on you.'

'I've been so angry with her,' I say. 'I almost can't believe it wasn't me who killed her. I've thought about it enough over the years.'

Vera does not look shocked. 'I admit I may have plotted her downfall a few times myself.' She shakes her head. 'She was a . . . difficult woman. I don't think you know the half of it. You will never be able to understand what Zelda and the others went through.'

She's right, of course. I know less than half of my mother's life, of the rupture she experienced. But Simone knows and so Vera must know more. It was not untold, then, my mother's story. She did not share the fate of so many other women, their voices silenced.

'The war never left us,' Vera says, turning now to stare out of the window. Rain begins to tip against the pane, gently at first, and then with more insistence.

'Neither of them ever spoke to me about the war,' I say, thinking of Samuel now. Both my mother and he so violently separated from their past, and for Samuel twice over, by his refusal to talk about it. 'My mother just alluded to it. Ramblings. Talk of blood. The rest was buried.'

Vera turns back to me, dark eyes watery now. 'No one wants to give it another life.'

'I only found out she had another husband yesterday,' I say, shaking my head. 'Did you know? I can't believe Zelda was such a heartbreaker.'

'No.' Vera's tone is sharp. 'Zelda's heart was broken. They broke her. They made her watch as they tossed her father and her husband in a mass grave. She was still a teenager. A girl.'

I gasp. Vera pales, suddenly sits up straight. Is it a kindness or a cruelty to share this detail? The image of my mother, young, tortured, hangs between us.

'*Ziskayt*,' Vera says. 'It must be very painful for you not to have been able to say goodbye. Not to have the chance to forgive her. Or to receive her forgiveness.'

And I can see that Vera means well, but I bristle, temper flaring again. It would, of course, be nice to open my heart and forgive all. But there are some things I've learned I'm not capable of forgiving. Or at least there is one thing I cannot forgive.

'I came from her body,' I find myself saying. 'She was *my* history. She severed me, erased me. She killed me off long before she did it to herself.'

Vera inhales sharply. I let my eyes flicker to her hands

again. She is wringing them, looping fingers through fingers. I can't stand to see it, her face so composed and then her hands giving everything away like that.

Silence stretches between us. A pigeon coos at the window. The rain has passed.

I finish the marble cake and then say, 'What was she like as an old woman?'

'She got fat,' Vera says finally. 'Enormous. *Oy*, she would have hated to die that fat.'

I know this is Vera's way of trying to show me that my mother was a real person with relatable and stupid problems. Because I haven't forgotten, of course, how my mother battled with her body, with its solidness and lack of waist. How she so desperately wanted to stay slim. And so I know it's true – Zelda would have hated dying fat.

'A fat corpse,' I say, shaking my head. And we are both laughing now. Not at my mother, not really. At the ridiculousness of it all. Because what would preoccupy our minds as we took our final breath? Not a grandiose flickering reel of milestones and precious moments, but rather the petty, earthly preoccupations we all fall prey to. And with this thought, I suddenly see the whole sad scene: my mother washing and dressing herself in her favourite outfit, her last meal, the bottles of pills on the kitchen table. Maybe the radio was on. A notebook beside her. Was she planning to write her final fuck yous but found the pencil lead blunt when the time came? How uncomfortable it must have been to swallow so many tablets, and with what – water? Sherry? Gin? Did she take one last look around the flat? Admire the décor which she never refreshed. All those shades of red, rippling now, swimming before her eyes. And then the walk to her bed, pulling back the sheets and getting in, laying her head on the pillow and waiting. Waiting. The mind waiting for an end, the body hanging on, that strong heartbeat weakening against its will.

My mother gave up. She'd really had enough this time.

How long did she spend picturing it, turning the image around in her mind? She must have mentally tested the idea endlessly, a toe dipped in bathwater – too hot, too hot. Might it have been the greatest feat of imagination she ever managed? To really, truly be able to imagine herself dead and then go towards it. She chose not to articulate her vison. No note – the detail that plagues my sister. But it *was* a communicative action. She didn't need to write a note. My mother took charge of her story by ending it.

'A fat corpse,' Vera repeats, giggling now at the audacity and the truth of the words. My mother would have laughed too. Whatever her shortcomings, she was not a woman without a sense of humour. She would have thrown back her head and roared. *Get that woman to Slimming World*, she'd say, *before she kills herself.*

Vera stops laughing. 'No matter her actual size, Zelda was always the kind of woman to occupy the whole room.' Solemn now, she leans so far across the table that I feel the warmth of her breath as she says, 'At some point one of you was going to have to let it go. She's dead now, Edie, so it's going to have to be you. You're going to have to let it go. Let it all go.'

She sits back in her seat, takes another bite of marble cake. 'You're an heir to her history, if nothing else. As close to a son as she ever got.'

And I hate her for that comment. I hate it.

To understand how to continue to live with Harry, I had to learn how to attend to his desires. These were not sexual: that part was mostly consigned for his wife. His house was an institution and there were unspoken rules. This institution would remain a refuge only if I understood the rules.

It took me some time to grasp the different world Harry had occupied since birth, the world of sons, not daughters. I had to learn that when a boy is born, he grows and thrives in a home made by a woman. It does not matter if his family is rich or poor, the mother meets his basic needs for food, warmth and safety and when these are established, she conjures and curates an environment where he can become the best man he is able to be. She facilitates his curiosity, his sense of play. She tells him his feelings are valid and how he must demand things of the world. And, as she narrates to him the story of his future successes, she washes and presses his clothes, changes his bedsheets, prepares his meals. He returns each day to a sparkling home where he is free to think and relax and to nourish himself before a good night's sleep.

After the nurture of his mother, Harry was sent to boarding school where he continued to avoid the laborious demands of keeping house. There were cleaners and cooks and a housemistress who could also serve as the object of his fantasies. Later, he acquired a beautiful wife who had been training for the role since she was born, and she picked up the baton from his mother and his housemistress with skills gleaned at a Swiss finishing school.

They moved to an enormous home in the countryside with many rooms to host many friends and she pored over catalogues and made calls to builders and painters and when he came home from work it was to an expertly cooked dinner and a hospitable and impressive home. At night, she offered him her hospitable and impressive body and he came home all over again.

Now Joanna was tired, or bored, and she passed the baton to me. The girl who paid no attention to her destiny as a *baleboste*. Who dreamed of more than facilitating the man in her life – who, in fact, could not comprehend having a man in her life at all. If only my mother had known how deep in dialogue I was with the girl she'd hoped I'd be. How she would have laughed and laughed.

In Harry's house I had a luxurious bedroom and en suite bathroom and all the food I could eat and all the wine I could drink. I walked the dogs, and when we dined at home I prepared the meals, and in the days between the cleaner's visits, I swept and I wiped and I dusted. I took care of Joanna's needs that Harry couldn't satisfy.

We still threw parties most weekends and I drove to

the shops for supplies: food and booze, condoms and lube. I made the call for the drugs and I paid the dealer with Harry's crisp fifty-pound notes. I collected the empty bottles from around the house in the days that followed. And, like Joanna, I offered my body to the people who filled our many rooms on Friday and Saturday and sometimes Sunday nights. In the half-dark, I accommodated their various shapes and the various shapes of their desires and I stretched myself to let them in.

I learned my duties but Joanna and I didn't add up for Harry. We were a situation, the three of us. A situation, not a unit. I was missing things, parts gouged out where Harry sought softness. I was not quite as pliable and helpful as he expected. I often performed my duties ineptly. I was not quite grateful enough. And so the spectre of a fourth person appeared in our tryst, a person entirely concocted for Harry and who I couldn't quite become. Her shadow followed me around, but it did not fit mine. The best parts of me, the best parts of Joanna – they had to exist combined somewhere, he thought. It was this woman Harry wanted. I saw him searching for her at parties. This fourth person was a long cool drink of water. I was the tequila shot you were bullied into drinking.

In the meantime, I made all his meals. I *was* a good cook.

Joanna's breath drags as she inhales her cigarette. I expected her to be annoyed I've decided to stay the rest of the week and help Simone clear the flat. Instead, she sounds relieved. I adjust the earpiece of my mother's ancient landline. I had to wipe face powder from the receiver before placing it to my ear. Now I can't stop thinking there are particles of my mother's dead skin on my fingertips.

Joanna blows out smoke. She announces that Stella and her husband are still fighting about his plan to move the family to Qatar.

Another pause. The cigarette fizzes.

'She's going to stay here for a few days, darling,' she says. 'Until things settle down.'

Now it's my turn to be relieved. Anything longer than twenty-four hours with Joanna's eldest daughter is unbearable. I tell her it's good Stella has her mother around for this rough patch, and then thank her for the flowers, deciding not to mention how they broke with Jewish custom. She finally asks about my mother's funeral. It's easy to summarise – quiet, unmoving, a little embarrassing.

I confess I wore the leathers and she lets out that deep laugh of hers. I don't mention Kiki. Not her appearance at the cemetery or the continuation of my portrait. Certainly not our trip to a club.

She asks how it's going with Simone and I lower my voice to say that actually it's lovely and I mean it. I enjoy my sister's company. Her sense of humour, her unflappable cool. I've promised Anais that I'll read with her this evening. Joanna's 'Hmmm' tells me that this is not what a person should be feeling after their estranged mother kills herself. Or perhaps it's ambivalence. I pause, wondering if I care what she thinks, and she fills the space with news that our neighbour Noreen is helping to walk the dogs. With this, my absence from Damson Manor is suddenly reframed as an inconvenience for Joanna. A sharp comment is about to escape my lips when I hear Simone swearing, so I excuse myself and promise to call later.

Simone is in my old bedroom. It's so full of junk I only recognise the red wallpaper. I whisper her name. She turns, several interlocked belt buckles in her hand. 'I thought you'd done another runner,' she says. 'Would you believe I've been trying to separate these for fifteen minutes?'

I believe her. She is flushed, sweating despite the cold. I take the belts, join Simone on the floor beside a bureau and explain about bumping into Vera and calling Joanna. It takes thirty seconds to separate the belts. I've no clue as to why it was even necessary. It's all heading to the charity shop.

Simone has very little to say about Vera and I realise

we must have different memories of the women of Carlton Mansions.

We continue sorting, decision-making. Items boxed. Relics face down. There is a pleasant rhythm to the folding, to making neat piles. But as my hands order the mess and more of my old bedroom reveals itself, I begin to feel uneasy. Returning to this building, I cannot fit the life I remember into its space. Time has flipped into a weird shape. It has no pattern. No logic. Decades have passed and yet they're rewinding as my sister and I unmake my mother's life. I drop a wedge of unopened tummy-control knickers into a bag and then stop, struck by sudden vertigo. Although I'm surrounded by my mother's life, her voice still hasn't returned.

I realise I've said this last thought out loud when Simone turns to stare at me. She is standing on a chair, tackling the wardrobe drawers methodically, one by one, as if the accumulation of objects could be tamed somehow. A lion's den of knickers. Through the window beside her, the sky is a silver mist. A spider scuttles across the pane. I open the nearest overstuffed drawer. I can feel her eyes still on me.

'All this red,' I say, for something to say.

Simone steps down from the chair. She gives me a serious look. To the good Jewish daughter, there can only be one thing wrong with me. 'Are you hungry?' she asks.

We take the Tupperware of potato salad and cold salmon and egg mayonnaise rolls to the kitchen. I wash the grime from my hands, dry them on my jeans. Simone moves around the cupboards and drawers instinctively. 'The food's always the same at shivas,' she says. 'Doesn't matter who's died – always variations on a theme.'

We take a seat at the table. I turn a fork over and over. 'This was always my favourite room,' I say.

'The only room that isn't red,' she replies.

I grin at her, then bite into a challah roll. Egg mayonnaise oozes. I taste my father's tortilla again. 'Was there something that she ate before she . . . ?' It is the first question I've asked about the night of our mother's suicide.

'A meal?'

'Yes, did you find a plate in here?'

Simone looks surprised and then shakes her head. 'I don't know. There was nothing on the table except her wedding rings. The last thing she did before she went to bed was take off her rings.'

Went to bed. A curious phrase, though an accurate one: it is where Simone found her body. We both look down at the table. I see my mother, old and fat and furious, forcing the two gold rings up and over a swollen finger. The sound of metal gently tapping against wood.

'Maybe her last meal was the takeaway at ours,' Simone says. 'Do you think it was the Chinese food that finally did it?'

I snort. 'A subpar spring roll?'

'Soggy seaweed?' Simone giggles and then forks some salmon into her mouth.

'What's odd,' I say, 'is that it's boring and creepy here at the same time.'

She shrugs. 'It's just what needs to be done.' She cuts another chunk of fish, pushes it onto a slice of potato. 'We've got to be patient. Zelda taught me a lot about patience.' She raises a brow. 'Accidentally, of course.' She examines a gloop of mayonnaise on the table. 'I read somewhere that Simone de Beauvoir thought women who were mothers had learned the discipline of patience to their detriment. *Fatal patience*, she called it. I wonder what de Beauvoir would have thought about our reversal of patience – daughter to mother.' She sighs. 'I was fatally patient with Zelda my entire life. I tried to protect her from herself. But to what end? She left me to discover her dead body.'

I blink at her words, so sharp, so unexpected, and then slide my chair towards her so that we are sitting side by side.

I recall my mother's darkest days after my father left, her solid body in the bath, washing her back, the hours spent in bed before Samuel entered her life, and she begins to shrink before my eyes until finally she is a child again. A lost girl. Hopes of youth destroyed, missed opportunities, persecution and flight, her mother's rejection, one murdered husband, abandoned by a second, a third's sudden death. I see it all so clearly now.

'Vera thinks I should let go,' I say. 'She thinks I need to forgive.'

'No shit,' my sister replies.

And this phrasing is so unlike Simone that I burst out laughing.

'I don't know how to do it. How to let go,' I say, gathering myself, 'because I never knew our mother. Not really. Her life has distilled into a few years for me. I had no idea she was even married before Sal.'

There is something hopscotch-like about how I've considered the story of my mother's life, choosing which squares to land on, which ones to avoid. But the squares I skip over are as much a part of the game as the ones on which I land. There are only so many times they'll tolerate watching the soles of my feet fly past. They demand to be acknowledged.

I share what Vera let slip about Odessa.

Simone's face turns grave. 'You don't want to know,' she says quietly. 'Not really. You got on with your life and you missed the worst of it. What's the point pulling up the past now? You were spared.'

Maybe Simone is right. I should be okay with a partial story. The memories I have are already too much, and yet I find myself saying, 'But how did we get here? How did we get to this?'

Simone is staring out of the window. A mist has replaced the rain. She turns and looks at me, and her eyes are wet. 'She talked about it for so long I never thought she'd actually do it. I thought it was hypochondria.'

'*Why bother getting up alive?* That's what she used to say.'

'No,' Simone says firmly, pushing her plate away. 'It was so much more than those old Yiddish sayings.'

She seems cross with me for the first time. 'You know

I didn't *leave*, Simone. She threw me out. I was sixteen. I had nothing.'

But if my sister hears me, she doesn't react. 'You missed the worst of it,' she says again. 'The unending melancholy, frayed nerves. She went completely downhill. Offended everyone and then drew a curtain around herself and disappeared. She didn't get out of bed for weeks. In perfect health but convinced she was dying of some ailment or other. No one knew what to do. Every attempt to rouse her failed. She was completely unreachable. Conked out on Valium. It was like living with a permanently shut door. She needed help. Finally, Dad had to admit her.'

'Admit her?'

Simone is silent. She reaches across the table, tears a piece of challah and rolls it into a ball between her fingertips. She looks so pale I begin to panic.

'Simone?'

She takes a breath and in a faraway voice picks up the thread of my mother's life from where I left it dangling more than thirty years ago. There was a wall around Zelda, she says, which only came down when her depression deepened, and when it abated, the wall went right back up. But when Simone was twelve, the depression stuck and the wall stayed down. Samuel was left with no option. She needed real help. More than he could give. And she was admitted to an asylum.

Samuel drove them to Barnet in his old Citroën. It was not in Zelda's nature to be coerced, so her acquiescence was as unsettling as the journey itself, where no one could bring themselves to speak. Zelda's silence after months of wailing and curses and threats was stunning.

The asylum was enormous, a series of huge red-brick buildings set among clipped green lawns with an enormous water tower in the distance. Samuel parked at the gate, instructed Simone to kiss her mother goodbye, then stepped around the car to open the door. Zelda had convinced herself she couldn't walk unaided, so he bent to scoop her from the seat, two hands slotted into her armpits, and they went unsteadily towards the entrance. Zelda's body, which had always dominated the rooms of Carlton Mansions, was now dwarfed by the complex of interlocked buildings. Until that moment, Simone had only been able to envisage an outline of what ailed her mother, but now the hospital provided a backdrop that fleshed out the problem by giving it somewhere to go.

As they drove home, Samuel explained that it was an esteemed place where her mother would receive the care she needed. In turn, they must be ready to receive her when she returned. So, while her mother spent six weeks on the ward at great expense, Simone learned how to budget the weekly groceries, to prepare food, how to chatter over dinner and discuss the day's events. No Zelda calling her name. No Zelda ignoring her name being called. No, her mother's voice was occupied, telling her story to the doctors at the clinic.

Simone looks up as if suddenly remembering I am here. 'I can't forget the blankness of her face,' she says. 'Such a contrast to my father's, which was lively and open to the world. What else could they do but shock her out of that way of thinking?'

'Shock her?'

Suddenly Lyra's youthful face appears before me. The convulsing and vomiting as images of naked women flashed across a screen. I freeze in my seat. 'Wait, they shocked her? With electricity?'

Simone's nostrils flare. 'She wasn't just a bitch, Edie! She was clinically depressed. Everything she did came out of that sickness. And the treatment worked. She came back so much better and for a while there was peace. But the effect didn't last. After a few months she was a shell again. Worse, maybe. Eventually, she went for another course of treatment. And this time when she came home there were days of complete vacancy. She barely recognised us. It was terrifying.'

I reach across the table and take her hand.

Simone's fingers grip mine tightly. 'My whole life has been defined by being her daughter.'

'Would you believe me if I said the same was true for me?'

'I would.'

'So what now?'

She squeezes my hand again before taking my plate and placing it on hers. 'Now? We empty this place of ghosts.'

Simone stood beside me at the kitchen window, arms folded across her chest, staring out at the garden. The damson tree was drooping with the last of its small, purple fruit. It was my job to pick them and make the jam Harry heaped on his morning toast. He had fired the gardener in some fit of uncalled-for rage and in the two months since, the grounds had taken on a subtle rebellion, growing at strange angles, stretching into spaces once forbidden. The white pampas grass had taken particular advantage of its freedom, bending and jutting out its feathery seeded heads as if in distress. A few flowerpots had smashed on the patio after a strong wind had swept through the night and no one had cleared the shards of terracotta. It was dawning on me that the garden would be allocated to my list of chores until Harry found the time or inclination to hire someone new.

I turned to face Simone and suggested we take a tour of the grounds after lunch.

'It's very peaceful here,' she said. Two blue tits had landed on the bird feeder. They pecked delicately at the seeds. She lowered her voice and dug me in the ribs. 'I'm not sure it suits you.'

I had barely recognised my sister when she arrived. She'd grown so tall, legs wrapped in tight flares, hair ironed into a straight brown sheet which reached her hips, the proud poise of someone newly married. Now she was free from our mother, living away from Carlton Mansions for the first time. The wedding had been a modest affair, just a few friends and Arnold's family. Our mother was still recovering from a mastectomy but had made the ceremony after her request for Simone to postpone it was not met. According to my sister, she did not smile much on the day. There had been no question of my attending.

By the time Arnold's car crunched along the driveway, Harry, Joanna and I had already drunk several vodka tonics. The three of us had been drinking more in general. I knew what Simone would think. We were a mess. But I'd spent the entire morning cooking, marinating lamb, shredding red cabbage, slathering potatoes in goose fat. I wanted so badly to recreate the Sunday lunches Simone and I used to enjoy in Primrose Hill when she was a teenager. As we ate, Joanna effortlessly played her role as hostess. She knew how to be gracious, how to drive a conversation. But when Arnold asked how long I'd been living in Broadstairs, Joanna replied on my behalf. 'Oh, years,' she said. 'Edie is *such* a good friend to the family.' I winced. Friend of the family. Family friend. Simone kept her eyes on her plate.

It didn't take long for Harry to start talking about his

new car – his new baby, as he called it. As he sweated and gesticulated, a purple vein throbbed at his temple. I watched it with curiosity. To his credit, Arnold seemed to be listening with enthusiasm – which was all that Harry asked of anyone, really. Arnold must have had good practice with our mother.

'What do you say, Simone?' Harry asked, his face bright and round. 'Can I borrow your new husband?'

Simone blinked. 'What for?'

Harry guffawed. 'A little spin around in the new Porsche.'

'It's *yellow*,' Arnold added with a wry smile.

Simone's gaze went to the empty bottles of wine on the table. 'Arnold, do you think—?' But Harry cut her off. Harry did not stand for hesitation. He was go, go, go. Get, get, get. His eyes had taken on the kind of whirling motion I'd learned to fear. He stood and clapped an arm around Arnold's back. 'This is going to blow your mind.'

There was no discussion, of course. There never was with Harry. Arnold shot his wife a conciliatory look and allowed himself to be led away.

After they left, Joanna took the dogs for a walk and I led Simone around the grounds. We linked arms and shared stories from our lives which felt different when expressed face to face. I realised how much the world was still going on without me.

'How do you bear him?' she asked.

'Harry? I drink too much.'

'But seriously.'

'Seriously. He's hardly here anyway. Away with work. Other women, too, I suspect.'

Simone shuddered. 'He gives me the creeps.'

I showed her the gardens. The pool. The aviary. The stables. I showed her such things we never had, could never dream of having, growing up. It was a good thing there was so much to see because after a short while I found I had very little news to share. My days were long, expansive, yet . . . there was nothing to say. Only when the sky began to take on that darkening navy hue did I realise how long the men had been gone.

'What time is it?' Simone asked. But I couldn't answer because I only owned my father's watch and I had put it away; it was still too painful to look at, even though years had passed since he'd left. We quickly walked through the orchards behind the house, leaves crunching underfoot. I saw Joanna's silhouette in the back doorway, smoking and worrying at her hair, before she saw us, and when I called out her name she squinted into the dark garden and then waved her arms about. I could hear her cursing. I knew immediately that something was wrong. Joanna never swore in front of company. Simone broke into a sprint and I followed her.

A dislocated shoulder. The car a write-off. We were lucky, really, that it wasn't worse.

Harry bribed the officer, or the magistrate, or whoever it was, and didn't lose his licence or do any work in the community because that was how the story went when you were rich, I learned.

I looked at Simone as she wrote down the name of the hospital where Arnold's shoulder was being checked and where Harry was being treated for concussion. She did not want to come with us. She refused over and over, and I said, 'Simone, I'm sorry, I don't know what to . . .' But then I tailed off. She was staring at me with such fury.

I kept waiting for her face to uncrumple and lift.

'What *is* this life?' she hissed.

It was a question I hadn't dared to ask myself.

Anais is reading aloud from the beginning of *Anne of Green Gables*. Knees tucked under her chin, her eyes follow the lines carefully, the nail of her little finger pressing against the previous pages, keeping them at bay. Her hair hangs in almost-dry strands down her back; her skin smells of clean oats.

Beneath us the giant green beanbag leaks, stuffing depleted, white polyester beads pooling on the floor. Those balls are a nightmare to hoover, staticky and impossibly small, giving chase across carpet. Kiki had a similar beanbag when she was younger and would throw her tiny body at it with such gusto that small splits appeared at the seams. Hours lost collecting the balls, stuffing them back in, sewing it all up again.

Anais is enamoured with Anne and her constant chatter and her optimism about her new home. She is charming, but it is her orphan status that thrills Anais's ten-year-old mind. No parents – a terrible possibility to consider. Anne is a character out of place. First she is forced to make a new home in a stranger's house, then she is forced to make her own home in the world. Unbearable sadness, countless dangers, and yet what potential it holds for self-fashioning! When Anais says the words 'orphan asylum child', a visible shiver goes through her body. She feels this way precisely because her own mother is so dependable. Imagining Anne's life takes Anais so far from her own it is like reading science fiction. There is no recognisable world without Simone.

Anais stops reading, stumbling over the word 'perturbation'. I suggest she has another go. She draws out the word, stretching it into its rightful four syllables. I've noticed that when she finds a word she doesn't know, she tries to shrink it, condense the sounds and get it over with. I don't want her to shrink the word, I want her to open it like an invitation. *It will take you somewhere*, I want to say.

Anne of Green Gables is one book of many on Anais's shelf that feature orphans. I remember reading the same ones at her age. In children's stories, discomfort and vulnerability give way to tenacity and, in the end, a happiness that compensates for a lack of parental love. Or so it seems. This was not my experience of being parentless in the world. Most of the characters inherit affluence and go on to live the life that was always waiting for them.

Anais yawns then, her mixture of milk and adult teeth gleaming.

'Maybe stop there?' We look up. Simone is in the doorway, the prettiest smile on her face.

Anais nods and puts herself between the ocean world

pattern of her sheets. She points at the sharks and whales and names each one of them for me. 'You should visit more,' she says finally. I remove the enormous velour bolster pillow, pull the duvet to her chin, and whisper, 'I know.'

Simone closes the door behind us. 'You're very good with her.' She pauses. 'Come on, the nine o'clock film's about to start.'

I follow her downstairs where Arnold hands me a large glass of white wine and pats the space beside him on the sofa. I sit, a little stiffly at first, and then tuck my knees under my chin, as Anais did, and rest against one of the cushions. The radiator behind me pulses with warmth.

Simone settles in an armchair and turns on the TV. It flickers briefly, blinking, caught in the static that appears moments before something new begins.

When I asked the question it was with the flippancy of new lovers. Joanna and I were no longer new, but going through a particularly good patch, the kind where you remember what drew you to each other in the first place and encounter it again with pleasurable surprise. It was mid-autumn. Leaves were rusting brown and the wind bit, but we were warm that morning, lazing in the Jacuzzi at Joanna's health club. No one else was around.

'What is your *best* thing?' I had asked, expecting her to talk about jewels or designers or some vase to which she was especially attached. I laid my head against the cool tile, flexed and unflexed my feet. Bubbles burst over my body. I thought she was deliberating over her choice until quietly she said, 'My brother.'

Joanna had never spoken about her brother. Once or twice Harry had raised the topic but she had shut him down so quickly it was as if it had never happened.

She didn't look at me as she spoke, but instead talked to the water. Louis was four years younger than her, she said. Born two months too early, he had been tiny with skin like skimmed milk. He'd spent those first few weeks hidden away in hospital and when she was finally allowed to see him again he had a little tuft of gold hair on the crown of his head that she adored. She covered his face with kisses until her mother dragged her away. 'I vowed to be his protector,' she said. 'When we were separated by my going to boarding school, I howled and howled. I wrote to Louis, not my parents.'

This sense of coming too early, too soon, never left him, she said. He was always overly alert, in a state of constant surprise at life – how it was waiting for him, ready to be embraced. It must have been so exhausting, this unending surprise, and as he grew older he became restless, agitated, angry. And then he began his metamorphosis into a succession of people she did not recognise.

She paused. The jets had paused too, and there was a terrible quiet.

'I saw some things in that time,' she said, speaking slowly, with care, 'things I could never have imagined witnessing, twisted situations he got himself into that clung to my mind like barbed wire. I do believe a lot of it was down to his schooling – which was impeccable, of course.'

She blinked several times. He'd had the finest education a young boy could receive from four years old, she said. But by the time he was an adolescent, his privileged environment came with its own specific set of problems. So while his housemasters raised his IQ and treated his mind with the utmost respect, Louis and his friends did the opposite with their bodies. Or perhaps that's not true –

they pushed the boundaries of their bodies. They had the resources for that kind of behaviour. Access to an unfathomable amount of cash. Much more than Joanna was ever given. And they used it to lose their virginity and they used it for drugs.

With Joanna, though, Louis was always gentle. When they were both home from the school term, he'd curl up like a cat in her lap and she would stroke his hair and listen to him talk. Of course she understood that everyone experiments, but Louis always liked it that much more than everyone else. It was an infatuation, strange not seedy. He was enamoured. But then he tried heroin.

'When he overdosed,' she said, 'I felt that my very skin was thick with grief. I was too heavy to get out of bed.' Joanna took a deep breath. 'Louis, even when he was at his worst, was my best thing. He was golden.'

There was a terrific whoosh of water as the jets started up again and just like that she snapped out of it. 'Let's get out of here, shall we? I promised Harry we'd bring back some medicine for that nasty cough of his.'

Joanna stood quite suddenly, water streaming from her body. Her ability to switch modes was astonishing. Out of the sentimental, into the controlled. She was very, very good at that. It gave me whiplash.

We didn't know then that Harry's cough was never going to get better. For weeks the whole house had echoed with it. The sound wet, sticky, like a man trying to breathe with a plastic bag over his head.

After his diagnosis, I avoided their bedroom for months.

Or maybe I'd been banned. In the few glimpses I caught, his body was shrunken and dried, already half abandoned. His spirit stared from his eyes as if stunned.

My God it took a long time for Harry to let go. He was on the verge of dying for months.

He left Joanna and the kids a small fortune, of course, but it was far, far less than they were expecting. To everyone's surprise, Harry had concealed a gambling problem. He'd blown through Joanna's family money, too. I couldn't help but remember Dov, Vera's ill-fated husband. It's only men you hear about gambling away their riches, confident they'll always come out on top, never women. Secretly, I suspected much of Harry's money had been squandered on cocaine.

I wasn't mentioned in the will. I wasn't even mentioned at the funeral. But Harry must have known that as long as I remained in Joanna's affections it would all filter down to me anyway.

Joanna and I started a new phase of our lives together. I wonder if it made him roll in his grave.

Kiki takes three steps back and flicks rust-coloured paint onto the canvas. Her approach this afternoon has been much more active, full of movement. She squints at the canvas, a smear of ochre paint on her cheek, biscuit crumbs at her feet. In the hour since I've arrived, she has obliterated an entire sleeve of custard creams, peeling the two layers of biscuit from one another, crunching the first, sucking the second.

I shouldn't really be here. Anais had a stomach ache and Simone left me at Carlton Mansions to pick her up from school early. I said I'd keep clearing out the flat but I couldn't stand to be there alone. Kiki laughed when I arrived at the studio. I was wearing Simone's clothes. She told me this is the last time she'll need me to model for her in person. She's been working on my portrait day and night, our encounters fresh in her mind, and is thrilled with how it's going. I'm less thrilled – not because of the portrait itself, I don't care how it looks, but because she's told Joanna we've been meeting to finish it. Apparently, this conversation did not go well. I wish Kiki had warned me. Now it looks like I've been sneaking around.

I turn Joanna's disapproval over in my mind as I lie on the couch and Kiki overrides my silence with chatter, narrating the story of her day. 'On my way here,' she says, 'I was walking behind a mum and her young daughter. The girl was maybe five or six years old and weaving along the pavement on a stabiliser bike, trying to cycle without help. Each time I went to overtake her, she swerved at the last second and went the same way. I was blocked. It kept happening and I realised we were locked in a kind of dance that the girl was completely unaware of. The mum finally clocked I couldn't pass and quietly guided the kid in a straight line so I could overtake them. Then she turned to me and said, "Sorry, she's got a mind of her own today." And I shook my head and said, "No. She's got a mind of her own *every day*."'

Kiki stares at me, paintbrush poised. She looks a little murderous. I'm not sure what I'm supposed to say. I find it hard to believe that she did anything other than murmur, 'Thank you,' and keep walking.

'Don't you think it's preposterous, Edie, to pretend children aren't autonomous beings?' she says. 'Or to wish otherwise? Because that's exactly how we got in this mess. You and me, I mean. Why are our mothers unable to accept we have minds of our own? Why the desire to strangle autonomy, to bend us to their shape?'

Kiki pulls my mother into the present tense. But I am done speaking about my mother in *any* tense. I think about Anais and Simone and say, 'Joanna simply wants better for you than she had for herself. It's the mother's impulse – so I gather.'

Kiki shakes her head. Her gelled hair doesn't move. 'Nope. She's just mad we're spending time with each other. She thought I hated you.'

'So did I.'

She grins and moves her paintbrush around the canvas again.

'The real reason Joanna is tough on you is because she doesn't approve of you dating both Chloe and Ryan. It's too close to the bone. You must be able to see that.'

Kiki wrinkles her nose. 'How can she begrudge me the same choices she made?'

I remind her it's because Joanna has never felt that she could be public with her sexuality. She doesn't know how to claim her choices. She doesn't know how to reconcile the way she was brought up with the person she actually is. I clear my throat. 'The word is repressed.'

Kiki grimaces. And then it's as if she's attacking the canvas, so violently does she apply the paint. Her whole body moves. I watch, impressed by her concentration.

It's getting dark outside but the studio's white tracking light makes it difficult to discern the hour. I try not to shiver. I wonder if I've gone too far calling Joanna repressed. Finally I say, 'I liked Chloe.'

'She liked you. She told me she'd no idea you were such a raging butch.' Kiki bursts out laughing and when she recovers says, 'You know what I'm struggling with? Your scalp.'

'My scalp?'

She nods. 'It's completely unknowable under all that hair.' She puts down her brush and with the new purpose that has consumed her today, walks to the back of the couch and then instructs me not to move. I haven't moved in an hour. Her hands roam my head, fingers insistent as they strive to pull away the curls. Her warm breath animates the top of my head and sends shivers through me.

She giggles. 'You have dandruff.'

I swat her hand away.

She laughs as she walks back to the easel.

'Can you finish the painting now?' I tease.

'Yes,' she says, 'now I know your scalp is whiter and bumpier than I thought it'd be.'

I tentatively touch my head.

'Don't move,' she warns.

I swear under my breath.

'It's strange how you haven't asked me anything about the painting,' Kiki says.

'I'm not sure I want to know.'

With a sly grin she says, 'An artist in your service is a good thing, Edie. If you were a man you would care. You would consider a portrait part of your legacy.' She pauses. 'I've been working on it every day since we started. I have this image of you in my mind all the time. You must have given it *some* thought?'

I have, I tell her, but rather than seeing my face, I imagine fleshy flowers, roots for limbs, shapes that grow from the earth. I see a landscape, not a person. The idea of someone looking at a painting of me and 'reading' my body the way Kiki describes artworks she admires is unbearable.

'Jesus, Edie,' she says.

'What I've been thinking about more is your tutor,' I confess, only now realising this to be true. 'The one who thinks you can't see women as they are. What does *he* know about how women see other women?'

With a certainty that surprises me, she says, 'He sees *everything* more clearly than I do.' She puts down the brush and stares at me and I can almost feel the energy leaving her body. I wait, and then she begins to explain how she's never sure how much of her style belongs to her. She is so stirred up by other artists that she finds their influence tramping its way through her work, leaving behind footprints. 'I absorb too much,' she says. And as if to demonstrate her point, she launches into a description of a short film by Mona Hatoum. In it, photographs of Hatoum's mother in the shower are superimposed with scans of letters they sent to each other while living apart. The mother's body is shadowy at first, Kiki says, then it comes into focus as she speaks openly about her feelings, her sexuality and her husband's objections to her daughter's intimate observation of her naked body.

Watching it, Kiki says, she felt the emotional ties between mother and daughter. But also the shared sense of loss, the rupture of displacement. 'I want to know how Hatoum managed to make a work that speaks of closeness and loss simultaneously.' She is talking to the canvas now, not me. Or at least, she is talking to the me on the canvas.

'Before I saw this video,' she continued, 'I thought Hatoum only used her own body in performance pieces. They were always a feat of physical endurance but they were silent. Hatoum never used her voice. So when I watched this video and finally heard her speak, something inside me opened and I knew I hadn't been listening to my own voice either.' She pauses again. 'You really don't care what your portrait looks like?'

'No. I don't. It's not personal.'

'Your lack of curiosity is worrying.'

I laugh but Kiki is serious. She puts down her paintbrush decisively. 'Field trip!' she announces. 'Let's go to the Tate. You need to start seeing things for yourself, with your past and your memories and your bias and what blinkers you. You're in desperate need of being surprised.'

I find myself agreeing. It has been so long since I went to an art gallery, to a museum, to the theatre or the cinema. What have I been doing in Broadstairs all this time?

Kiki cleans her brushes, changes her shirt. I stretch my body. Joints pop. I pull Simone's grey sweater over her shirt, then slip on my leather jacket. We go out into the rain.

On the Harley, I tuck the ends of my hair beneath the helmet. Kiki's body is familiar to me now and I slot comfortably into the groove of her back. She drives so fast I have to close my eyes, my insides turning fluid as wind and water drown out the city sounds.

When we pull up outside the back of the Tate, it takes

a few moments for my stomach to settle. Kiki watches me impatiently. 'You're not old yet,' she says, and grabs my hand, tugging my arm the way a little child might, wanting to show me a frog she has found or a really good hole she has dug. *Come look, come look.*

We round the side of the building until we reach the river entrance, climb the imposing staircase and go straight to the Turner Prize exhibition. I'd imagined she wanted me to see Emin's *My Bed* but instead she leads me past that crowd and into one of the connecting rooms.

It's dark. We join the small audience in front of a pair of floor-to-ceiling screens which are set at right angles so that it feels like I'm entering the pages of an open book. The two screens are divided again to project four different images. The camera's eye roves across abandoned rooms but I don't know what I'm looking at until I turn away and read the text. The video is called *Gamma*, made by two sisters, Jane and Louise Wilson. It was shot in the former United States Air Force base in Berkshire. In 1979, NATO decided to station ninety-six cruise missiles there, a decision that gave rise to the Women's Peace Camp, a non-violent, anti-nuclear mass protest which is still going on.

I turn back to the screens. Now I see the abandoned base, its control panels, places to shoot missiles. There's a sense I'm watching something I shouldn't, that I'm an unwitting participant in someone else's dare as they trespass – I'm trespassing twice.

But the base is not as derelict as I thought. Flashes of

two uniformed female figures prowl the corridors. Their appearance assaults me. I'm the watcher being watched right back. And then I become aware of the low hum of working equipment. The first flickers of paranoia lick at me. Cocaine memories rise up, pranging and tugging at my consciousness.

'Disorientating, isn't it?' Kiki whispers in my ear. Her breath smells of biscuits. I murmur yes. No one else is in the room now. It is just us, side by side, staring at the images. And then she takes my hand in hers, a squeeze so gentle it would be imperceptible if she weren't pushing my ring deeper into my skin. Her skin is smooth like her mother's. I feel her body take a breath and in a small but firm voice she says, 'Joanna has a boyfriend. They've been together for years. His name is Jake. He's married.'

I keep my eyes forward, fixed on the projection. The colours swirl, blur and shift about the screen.

'That's where the money comes from,' she says. 'He gives her some kind of allowance. Daddy's cash ran out ages ago.'

There's a sudden burst of noise from the projection: too loud, too close. What is it? A woman crying out? I watch as the space becomes a labyrinth. My breathing quickens. I try to focus again on what I can see, to order the images in front of me. But each screen simultaneously depicts two different viewpoints, the same physical space from different perspectives. Sometimes I'm on the ground, sometimes looking down from above. It's like I have two sets of eyes. I'm unmoored, unable to really locate myself. I walk to the other end of the room to see if it makes a difference. But no. I return to the centre. There is no secure viewing position, no anchor.

'Edie,' Kiki whispers. 'I'm so sorry. I couldn't bear you not knowing a minute longer.'

I keep looking at the video and slowly the murky forms reassemble themselves. Two shapes. A mouth. One eye, then two noses. But they don't return to their original positions. Lips papered over cheek, eye on chin, nose on forehead.

A scrambled face.

Finally, I say, 'Is Stella staying at the house this week?'

'I don't know.'

I look back at the screens. Two women appear and then disappear again.

After Harry died and the kids had gone back to their lives, I took care of Joanna through her grief. I made her smoothies for breakfast, a salad for lunch, a proper cooked dinner. For a while we stopped drinking at lunch-times and took long walks together across the beach with the dogs. Some of Joanna's hard edges softened, soft as the perfectly draped clothes she wore every day for me, for herself, for no one. But we soon fell back into the old ways. Being a little wine-drunk was part of being sensual. Being a little dominant was all Joanna knew.

I had spent longer living with Joanna than I had with any person in my life, including my father and my mother. With Harry gone, we took to sleeping in the same bed. She clung to me, peppermint breath at night, sour milk in the morning. And whereas I had balked at this notion before, used to sharing my body with many bodies, thinking it banal, repetitive, to lie with just one, I was now awakened to the pleasure of the familiar, of the unremarkable fact of her face every morning, every evening. It was a new, less dramatic, joy.

We had still never held hands in public.

What belongs to me at Damson Manor? No furniture. No art. No mementos. The dogs are not mine, not technically, though I've been responsible for their upkeep. All I can lay claim to are the small raised marks on the wall where I've filled holes with Polyfilla. Recently painted windowsills which still bear the cracks of past use. The clever arrangement of Joanna's shoe boxes in the wardrobe. A bottle of shampoo for curly hair, serum to banish frizz. All things that can be emptied, undone, erased.

There is only that one trunk with photographs, my father's watch, an expired passport.

I don't know who Joanna is. I don't know what I am to her.

'Edie, what's the matter with you?' Simone asks. 'You've been folding and unfolding the same sweater for five minutes.'

We are cross-legged on the carpet of our mother's bedroom, a pile of her clothes between us. It is the fourth day of sorting our mother's flat and we've finally braved this room. I'm not sure if I expected to feel her ghost hovering above the bed, telling me off for trespassing, but in any case, she's not here. It is just another room, one full of too many things, like the rest of the flat.

In my hands is a red cashmere crew-neck sweater. The label says Marks & Spencer, size XL. I hold it up. The thing is enormous. And then I pull it over my head, slip my arms through the sleeves. It is far too big but the fabric is pleasing, luxurious. Something scratches at the back of my neck. A tag. It has never been worn.

'Are you losing it?' Simone jokes.

'It's likely.'

She points at the sweater. 'The two of us could fit in there.'

I nod, roll onto my knees and then pull the hem of the sweater away from my body. 'Come on.'

Simone giggles. She crawls over, turns to face the same direction as me, and then ducks her head under the fabric. Her body is much smaller than mine and as she wriggles her way up, the sweater stretches to accommodate her shape. Her hair rubs against my belly then my chest. She is a stream flowing towards the mouth of a river and as she strains to fit through the neck opening, we labour together in the name of Marks & Spencer, in the name of all the unworn red cashmere – no, all the unworn sweaters – until finally we merge as one and her head pops out in front of mine. 'It's our birthday!' she announces.

My sister's bottom presses against my thighs, her back squashing my breasts. It's cosy. I'm finally warm. We have changed the ecosystem of Carlton Mansions, which is always cold no matter how we blast the thermostat. We rock from our knees to the back of our heels, giggling as we try to stand. But we cannot make our limbs work in tandem. We keep falling backwards, my hands dashing out behind us to take our weight. We struggle, we laugh some more, we keep trying to stand, we want to make it work.

'On my count,' Simone says. She begins with 'three' and when she reaches 'zero' we move as one, foot in front of foot, four calves straightening, two spines unfurling.

We're up. We catch our breath. In and out. In and out. We're facing our mother's bed. We have not touched the sheets.

'How did we survive this house?' I ask the back of her head.

Simone shrugs and the movement lifts my shoulders with hers. No more thinking, our shoulders say.

And then she folds her arms behind her so that they wrap around the small of my back in a backwards hug, and I say, 'Joanna is cheating on me.'

For a moment Simone is silent. Then she squeezes me tighter. 'Forgive me,' she says, 'but aren't you . . . open?'

'Not since Harry died. I thought it was just us.'

'Another woman?'

'Another man.'

'Oh,' Simone says. 'Somehow that seems worse.'

'It is,' I say. And then I laugh. 'Fucking hell. Fucking Joanna. I didn't have a clue.'

'Fuck her,' Simone says.

'Fuck her!' But saying it out loud cements the image. Joanna has another lover. Another partner. A rich man. A rich married man. I thought we were growing old together, growing up – but she found another Harry. Nothing has changed in over twenty years. I have no job prospects, no money, and no claim on anybody.

We are still facing our mother's bed when Simone asks what I'd like to eat for dinner tonight.

I realise I'm smiling when her hair tickles my mouth. 'Why don't I cook?'

'*Can* you cook?' she asks.

'I'm excellent.'

'Well then, you can cook every night.'

Every night. The words open up a space inside of me. I feel Simone waiting.

I have not known what it means to make a family home. My mother's home was not hospitable; Joanna's home was so hospitable that strangers became intimates and then people who mostly faded from memory. Simone's home seems so normal.

'Okay,' I whisper.

There is a tremendous rip as Simone's head disappears and she disengages from the sweater. She turns to face me, grinning, and lightly touches the sweater's torn neck. 'Do you think we'll ever finish clearing this place out?'

The room is still a tip. But I think we will.

We go back to our task, energy renewed. We strip the bed silently. It is just a bed.

I find Zelda's diaries in a suitcase. There are so many.

All leather, colours changing over the years. I open the pages, flick through hungrily like the answers to the question of my mother's life might be contained inside. But it is a folly, I know it's a folly. Her diaries are filled only with appointments. Dentists, doctors, birthdays, anniversaries. Films seen. Dinner reservations. No emotions. And all of a sudden, I realise how strange it is that we haven't found any photographs or letters anywhere. I ask, and Simone tells me they were all burned during one of our mother's depressive episodes. She's not sure which one. So then, we'll not find any words from our mother or our fathers. No answers, no explanations. But we are dredging up what's left of the past. And we are unearthing a story. We are writing it together as the hours pass and the flat changes shape, somehow swelling with its new freedom, with potential.

'Don't kill me,' Simone says, flicking on the light switch as the room succumbs to the dark, 'but red is kind of your colour.'

I look down and realise I am still wearing the cashmere sweater. I laugh. Perhaps I've been wearing the wrong colour all along.

I thought about leaving Damson Manor many times. My imagination never stretched to where.

One night, Joanna saw it on my face. She coaxed it out of me. We were in the kitchen. I had a glass of red wine in my hand which I was gripping, knuckles paling.

What skills did I have? she spat. What education? How would I look after myself? *I needed her.*

I listened and I agreed and I was aware, so aware, that I was ignoring a strange sensation in my body, like someone had sliced me open in the night and moved my spleen just an inch to the left and then sewed me back up again. Ostensibly, nothing had changed. Yet.

How to account for the passing of time. I had woken up middle-aged. My stomach spread, hips wider. Skin a little rougher, a little redder. Everything took just that little bit longer.

To Joanna, I said, 'I've realised that we have absolutely no control over the person we end up becoming. I was so sure I would never be anything like my mother. And it happened so slowly I didn't notice until it was too late.

Look at me.' I was shaking. 'I'm a housewife. Not even a housewife.' I drained the wine. 'I wonder why it is,' I said, 'that you can have all the best intentions and still fail at even the simplest of tasks.'

Joanna didn't talk to me for two weeks after that.

Simone drops me at St Pancras after we take the last of the boxes to the charity shop. The furniture will be collected by the auction house. We have kept only the silver candlesticks which Zelda's mother, our grandmother Sonya who we never met, carried with her on the boat as they fled Odessa. They will live above Simone's fireplace. One small piece of history larger than either of us can really comprehend.

She kisses my cheeks goodbye and wishes me luck. I almost laugh.

I have a window seat on the train and I watch as minute by minute the city makes herself smaller, the buildings becoming diminutive as we pick up speed. How quickly suburbia arrives and all that green announces herself. The carriage is crowded, loud with the cheer of a Sunday afternoon in December. I forgot to bring a book. I fidget. I drink from a miniature bottle of wine. It sours my mouth.

When Simone and I found the silver candlesticks, I turned them over in my hands, feeling their smoothness. For thirty years, I hadn't thought beyond each approaching day and for the last two weeks I've thought only about the past. That was my scheme: I simply regarded the future like a moving carousel I didn't dare jump on.

Outside, the air smells like snow and salt, the sky white and threatening. The bus from Broadstairs station is infrequent and I wait in the cold with two pensioners and a teenage couple who cannot stop touching other. The girl sits sideways on the boy's lap as if he is about to stand and carry her across the threshold. As he kisses her neck, her small feet pedal the air with delight. The older women avert their eyes but I cannot look away.

The bus is slow, swollen with passengers who are deposited and replaced two-fold as it winds through the narrow grey streets. We pass chip shops, junk shops, Chinese takeaways and pubs. Terraced houses, detached houses, schools and then out into more green.

I get off and spend the short walk to Damson Manor organising my thoughts. Jacket zipped up tight, breath half frozen in the air, but I don't rush. I've only been gone a week but the road looks new to me again. It is beautiful here, the grand houses set back from the street, the careful landscaping, towering trees with their winter branches like telephone poles. In warmer months, a parade of rhododendrons, lavender, wisteria. The sound of reckless sprinklers. Fruit-laden jugs of Pimm's set down on metal garden tables.

I round the street and there is Damson Manor, rising out from behind the gates at the end of the road. From where I'm standing, it's impossible to tell its size, how much land surrounds it, how it stretches out, tentacle-like. Assertive.

I press the code to the gate and it swings open. The sky is already darkening but not one window glows with light. And then I notice – no car in the drive. The house looks abandoned. Weathered stone, peeling paint, a dying garden. Water drips thickly through the foliage.

The gravel crunches beneath my feet, which usually sends the dogs racing to the door. I wait for the sound of paws skittering across hardwood floors but it doesn't come. When I turn my key in the lock, I still expect to hear their panting, little yips of happy greeting. Instead, an empty hallway. It's freezing. I call out, 'Joanna?' And then, 'Mitzi, Coco, Betsey?' I don't believe she has taken all three out by herself. The quiet is heavy. I cannot remember the last time I've been here without the dogs.

I turn on the heating, wander through the house. Each room is full of deep corners which swallow up the dark. I flick on all the lights. The winds have started up and they shake the windows. Upstairs, I open each of the bedroom doors, looking for Stella, before finding myself in the kitchen again. She was never here. *Of course* she was never here.

I take a seat. Get up. Sit back down in another chair. I can't shake the feeling I'm not alone: every detail of the room speaks of Joanna's presence, from the plush velvet banquette to the marble countertop to the vase of powder-pink roses on the table. But I am alone. Not even my mother's voice comes to me anymore.

I loiter by the kettle. Make a pot of coffee, lace it with brandy, and then turn on the radio. Christmas songs.

Now what?

I wait.

She will come back.

Meanwhile, I decide I will cook. I will cook a hearty homecoming dinner and we will talk.

The fridge is empty save for condiments, butter, lemons and several apples. Joanna does not like to shop for food. But the freezer is full. The freezer is always full. I open an icy drawer, pick through the frozen packages. There is Ryan's venison, divided into portions. Joanna must have moved it from the fridge. I place one of the packages on a plate, set the microwave to defrost, and then it comes to me – I'll make dumplings. Nothing could be more comforting on a cold December night. My grandmother, Sonya, taught my mother how to make pelmeni and it is the only dish I know for certain that has been passed down through my migrating matriarchs. They should be made with beef or pork but I'll make do with what I have.

The preparation of pelmeni requires time and a few tricks. I set about making the pastry. My mother's thick hands were never more capable than when she was kneading dough, her wedding ring, the one my father gave her, pushed down over swollen knuckles. Joanna has a pasta roller, another gift from Harry that only I have used. I heave it out from the back of a cupboard, work the dough with my hands until it's sticky and then feed it into the roller. I test myself: how thin can I get it before it breaks?

When the venison has defrosted, I dice the flesh with my sharpest knife, piling it up and turning the chopping board at regular intervals until I'm left with mincemeat. I season it with salt, pepper and onion powder and fry the lot in a cast-iron pan until it's fragrant and tender.

Something trembles at the window. Sleet, coming down hard.

I use the base of a wine glass to cut circles from the dough. Place a teaspoon of filling into the centre of each one, run a wet finger around the outside edges, and then fold so that the meat is enclosed. I lightly pinch the delicate half-moon shapes. The dumplings taste better fried but I boil them anyway, like my mother would, like her mother would.

I set the table: two mats, two china plates, silverware, two wine glasses. I uncork a bottle of Burgundy, pour myself a healthy measure.

When twenty-five minutes have passed, I plate up, arrange the dumplings and drizzle them with oil and some chopped parsley from one of the pots on the windowsill. They should be served with sour cream but we will have to do without.

I take a seat and I wait. Click off the radio. They really are the most attractive pelmeni I've ever made. It would be a shame for them to go cold.

When I hear the key in the door, I realise part of me has been expecting this to be a folly. To eat the entire plate. Drain the bottle of wine. I force myself to remain still and listen for the familiar sounds. Joanna's keys dropping into the dish on the ottoman. The shake of the umbrella. The rustle of her coat as it's shrugged off. For the first time I consider Joanna might not be alone. But it is just her voice I hear when she calls out hello.

'Edie? Is that you?'

'In the kitchen.'

Joanna's heels click across the hardwood. I smell Shalimar before I see her and when she enters the room, she looks peaceably incurious. 'You came back early. I wasn't expecting you until Monday.' She glances at the kitchen table, smooths down her black sweater and then her shining blonde bob. 'What's all this?'

'Dinner,' I say. 'Sit.'

'How thoughtful.' Joanna slides into the seat opposite me. She leans across the table and kisses my mouth. Her lips are plump, recently glossed. Her breath smells of cigarettes. 'You must be tired after your journey.' Her eyes flicker as she takes in the dumplings.

I explain they are something my mother, and her mother, used to make. Joanna nods solemnly. 'How are you feeling?'

I pour her a glass of wine. 'Has Stella left already? Is that where you've been?'

'Hmm, yes,' Joanna says. 'She's going to work on things with Kamil.'

'And the dogs?'

Joanna looks at me blankly.

'Where are they?'

'Oh,' she says. 'I had a dog minder look after them this weekend. Too much, with Stella here and everything. I'm picking them up tomorrow morning.' She looks around. 'Gosh, it's hot in here.'

It's impossible to tell if she's lying. There is not one tic that would give her away. Has she spent the weekend with her lover? Have they been ordering room service in some expensive hotel? I serve us both a helping of dumplings. The steam has evaporated but they're still warm. I take a bite. The meat is juicy, perfectly seasoned. Joanna lights a cigarette. She does not touch her plate.

I gesture at the dumplings and explain they took ages to make. Surprised, she tells me I shouldn't go to such lengths. It is about care, I tell her.

She gives me a small, conciliatory smile and nibbles at one. 'Delicious, darling, thank you.'

And then I say, 'Who is Jake?'

The silence is almost nice. The longer it takes her to answer, the longer my question, my accusation, can remain unfounded, the answer untrue. It is the nicest silence I've experienced in a long while and I languish in it while Joanna decides how she wants to play this. Emboldened, I pick up another dumpling with my fingers, squeeze the pastry case, eat it whole.

Joanna watches as I chew. She takes a long, measured drag of her cigarette. Blows out the smoke. 'Why are you bothered, darling?'

I hold her gaze. A flush spreads across her cheeks. It must be clear who told me. 'Why am I bothered?'

She tips ash into the tray. 'Yes.' She shrugs. 'It's nothing new.'

'It's new to me.'

But Joanna is defiant. She raises her eyebrows just a little, an expression of innocence so practised, so bloody convincing, that all my fury comes at once. 'You're cheating on me!'

She takes several more puffs of her cigarette before she speaks. 'I'm doing nothing of the sort.' Another long pause. 'Did you think I was simply going to *wilt* into old age?'

I had expected this. A non-reaction. A downplay. But I'm defeated by her finishing-school poise, unable to control my voice the way she does and when I say, 'Joanna!' it is shrill, outraged.

She puts out the cigarette and folds her arms across her chest. Her hands are ivory-white, creamy. 'Darling, you're being childish. Where do you think the money comes from? And since when did we quibble over sex? It's really none of your business.'

'Then why keep it secret?' I spit.

Joanna considers me and I see that she is noticing Simone's clothes for the first time. She lets her arms drop to her sides and then lowers her voice to a growl. 'I let you into *my* marriage. I let you into *my* home. *My* bed. I gave you your life. And now this sullenness. This petulance. Don't be so ungrateful.'

I don't know what to say, paralysed by shame. I learned to expect, and accept, certain losses from my life with Joanna. But in an instant, I am reduced entirely. I am nothing but service.

She leans forward, lays her hands flat on the table.

'Now tell me, Edie, what have you been doing with my daughter?'

I bare my teeth. 'What a weird, horrible question. What a fucking terrible *thought*.'

'Whatever you are doing disgusts me,' she hisses. 'The both of you. You're disgusting.'

'There is nothing going on with Kiki, do you hear me? She's been my friend.'

'Christ, listen to you. *My friend.* You're not twenty anymore.' Her eyes glitter. Her flush deepens. She takes several breaths and then drinks deeply from her glass. The wine does its work. She gathers herself, draws back. 'Can we just leave it now?'

'What do you mean, leave it?'

'Let's talk about something else.' She picks up the nibbled dumpling and eats it. Her nose wrinkles a little. 'Tell me more about your sister.'

'Okay,' I say. 'I'll leave it.' I stand. I walk up the stairs to our bedroom and I drag a chair to the wardrobe and then I pull down my trunk. It hasn't been touched for a decade and it's covered in a thick layer of dust. I brush it off and listen for Joanna's footsteps, which do not come.

She is smoking when I return to the kitchen, staring straight ahead. She blinks when she sees me and then sighs like I'm a bluffing child who must be endured. 'Come on, Edie. Enough now.' She speaks slowly, like I might not understand. She watches as I pick up the trunk.

'It's all I'm taking,' I say.

I go to her then and gently place my hot forehead

against her cool one. I stay for a moment, skin on skin. Inhale her scent, her warm, smoky breath.

There's a line from my feet to the door. All I have to do is consider the line. All I have to do is consider my body. Extend along the line. Let my body extend along the line. Follow it. Extend my limbs. Stretch them. Reach out. The door. One foot follows the other.

Now Joanna's heels do click behind me.

Her overnight bag is by the ottoman.

'Edie,' she says, 'what are you doing? Come back here. Don't be silly. We need one another. We're a team, you and I. A team.'

But I don't turn. No last glance. I will not risk becoming a pillar of salt. Instead, as I step out into the night, I allow myself to briefly close my eyes. I see Joanna curled up on the sofa with a glass of wine, flicking though fashion magazines. I see the dogs running ahead of her as she throws a ball – never quite far enough for their liking. I see her sleeping on her side, breasts resting on one another. Blonde hair messy on the pillow. Mouth ajar. I see her eyes opening, blue irises slowly focusing on mine.

I arrive at Kiki's studio exhausted, an hour before Simone will come and pick me up.

Kiki pulls me into a hug. 'Well done,' she whispers and then draws back, smiling. 'Now close your eyes.'

She guides me through her studio, a cold hand on my shoulder. I keep walking, tentative, careful.

'Are you peeking?' she asks.

I shake my head.

We take a few steps forward and when she says, 'Now open,' she is standing by my portrait, showing me myself.

She has painted just my body and the chaise. There is no room behind me, only inky blankness where the drapes of my top float like a black waterfall, like the Black Sea, black curls nesting around my head before disappearing. She has taken me away from Damson Manor altogether.

The woman, I know, is me. The woman, I know, is paint. Time folds and all my selves, one for each year, spill out of that body. Here are all my years. Here are all my yearnings.

The chaise is foregrounded so as to create the sensation

that my body looms above me. I have a child's point of view. It pulls me into the centre, into my face. The nose protrudes, the mouth protrudes, the gap between my teeth just visible. My features are taking a stand. But it is the skin that dominates with its swathes of raw, burnt earth, umber and sepia. My body in yellow ochre, splashes of orange. There is fire in my limbs. There is fire in my belly. There is so much appetite. And in the shapes of my face my story, my mother's story. Our joint torpor. Zelda was a young girl when troops invaded Odessa. I'll never know what memories of this time remained with her through her life. So instead, I try to imagine my mother at fifteen, a year before her life, and mine, changed forever. I want to animate that young woman and keep the memory of her with me, even if it is, by design, a false memory. This young Zelda would have been very handsome. Already tall, already heavyset. The dark hair which I always knew to be short running down her back in a girlish braid secured with a red ribbon. Full mouth painted, the faint lines from nostril to upper lip unaware of the great crevasses they'll become. I have a home in that young body. The promise of me was with her at that time. And I want to tell her I am sorry for the life she was born into and then for the life that she chose to live and I see that her story is mine and mine is hers and we backed our narrative into a corner.

I go closer. And then I see: the black space is for me to step into.

I suffer a sudden vertigo so deep it's as if I am upside down.

'What do you think?' Kiki asks as she comes to stand beside me.

I see the person Kiki imagines me to be. Their face, their torso, their limbs. At once alien and recognisable. That her body has painted my body becomes a surprise intimacy. How could I not have considered this in all the hours we spent looking at one another. In that time, I have been reshaping my past in my memory but not imagining the future. What shape does it take? What shape *can* it take when the future forms itself from the stories we have told ourselves of the past?

It occurs to me that I could open the frame, extend that black space. There could be another way, another way of living.

I still haven't answered Kiki. She adjusts the question. 'What will you do now, Edie?'

When I answer, I talk to the woman on the wall before me. She is listening. I am listening.

Acknowledgements

Thanks to my writing family, whose insight and generosity I'd be lost without: Lucie Elven, Emily Ruth Ford, Sophie Kirkwood, Eve Kraicer, Philly Malicka, Natasha Randall, Jane Saotome and Tom Watson. To everyone at Borough Press with special gratitude to Sophia Schoepfer for her vision and dedication. To my agent, Seren Adams, for her wisdom and friendship.

To M & T for their love and support.

And to AO, for everything, always.

About the Author

Gemma Reeves is a writer and teacher who lives and works in north London.